THE CULMINATION OF EVERYTHING

A SUGAR VALLEY NOVEL

CHRISTINA C JONES

CHAPTER ONE

"*Two roads diverged in a yellow wood,*" I muttered to myself, stopping at a break in the heavily wooded path. It was still spring, the foliage full of ripe green hues, not yellow. And... there weren't exactly *roads* at the end of the fork I currently faced. There was a densely grown trail on the left, and its twin lay on the right, both calling to me with a chorus of birds and bugs, both illuminated by bright yellow sunlight peeking through the canopy of trees.

A decision to make.

Which was fine.

I was *great* at those.

Whipping out the neatly folded map from the pocket of my cargo shorts, I carefully traced my finger along the path I'd already taken. Pencil marks covered it – my personal, time-stamped notes of the landmarks I'd already passed on the three-mile hike. When I reached the illustration of the fork where I found myself now, I followed the left tine first, noting that it led over a bridged creek, and on to a picnic area, which I wasn't looking for yet.

The right side – heh. The *right* side. – led to my destination, a path further up the mountain, to a small runoff of the massive Sugar Leaf Falls.

I'd tackle *that* monster another day.

For now, I was almost at my destination, so the choice was an easy one. Not until I tucked the map back into my pocket did I noticed the—somewhat overgrown–signage that indicated precisely where the differing paths led.

To picnic area.

To falls viewing area.

Hooking my thumbs around the straps of my backpack, I chuckled to myself. *At* myself.

"Nice observation skills there, Kyle."

I ducked my head to avoid a low-hanging tree limb, continuing my trek through the lush greenery of the forest. In such surroundings, imagining myself as some brave adventurer, forging a previously uncharted path through the dense woods came with ease. A deep inhale of the unsullied fresh air brought a grin to my face, even as a light drizzle of rain carried a fine layer of moisture to my surroundings.

It didn't matter that my neat French braids would turn into a frizzy mess, or that my brand-new, purchased-just-for-this-trip hiking boots were going to get muddy. And I only minded a little that my cell phone might get a bit soggy.

I'd probably abandon it as a distraction before this "sabbatical" of mine ended anyway. What *mattered* was, at the end of it all, I walked away better than I came.

What, exactly, defined *"better"*?

Well... I was still working on that part.

I picked my way carefully along the trail, the sounds of picnicking hikers fading into the background music of the forest. For a few minutes, that "drizzle" of rain turned into a downfall steady enough to add to the composition, dripping from trees and drumming against the rocks, making me glad for the poncho I'd tucked within easy reach.

With my rain protection on, I pressed forward, undeterred. Impromptu or not, I had every intention of reaching the finish line for this hike, crossing it off the list of what I could accomplish. In my head at least, the quiet victory would make the long, hot bath I planned to take tonight even sweeter... assuming my lodge was ready by that time.

It hadn't been when I arrived.

That little check-in mishap prompted today's hike, and the teenager at the desk had been sweet enough, apologetic enough, that I didn't mind. I hadn't had plans inside the cabin anyway, other than possibly cracking open a bottle of wine.

This was better.

Without checking my map, I could tell my destination was near. The signature melody of birds and bugs grew faint in favor of the rush of water against rock, the trees became more and more sparse, overtaken by the presence of natural stone, and quite suddenly... I'd arrived.

And it was... *breathtaking*.

One of the higher mountain peaks spread out before me, towering into the sky. It wasn't a significant drop—just nineteen feet according to the notation on the map I'd picked up at the lodge before I'd embarked. Still, it was enough height that the stream—a runoff from Sugar Leaf River – created an impressive waterfall which fed into a large natural pool before running off the side of another cliff that would lead the water back to join the river.

I stepped in closer, feeling a soothing sort of calm as I took it all in. The rain had stopped, the sun was back out, and the foliage seemed especially lush, probably due to the proximity of the water.

It was... *quiet*.

3

Not *silent*, not with the water and the birds and the bugs and whatever else lurking in the shade of the trees, but there was an undeniable serenity that wrapped itself around me, laying heavy on my skin.

Foreign.

So much so I had to force myself into stillness, into not fidgeting. Into sitting with a feeling that had eluded me for a while now.

Peace.

Today was a lucky one, according to the teenager at the front desk of my lodge rental. It was an odd time of the month, odd day of the week, odd time of day, so I had this all to myself. Maybe for an hour, perhaps a few minutes, I didn't know.

But I had *this* moment.

I pulled my cell phone from the safety of my pocket, bringing up the camera. I snapped a few pictures of the view, then tapped the button that would access the front-facing camera. With the waterfall, pool, rocks and trees behind me, I grinned at my image – fuzzy braids peeking from underneath the hood of my bright yellow poncho, framing my reddened face.

Perfect.

I snapped that picture, then moved closer to the water, planting my feet on the slick rocks to make sure I was balanced before I lifted the camera to snap another. I was at the edge of the short cliff that led down, closer to the main waterfall, so I decided to snap a picture there, too. Once again, I planted my feet for a secure base, then raised the phone, framing the picture like I wanted before I moved my thumb to the shutter button.

And then *something* came darting out of the woods.

The sudden movement forced a startled *"Ahhh!"* from my lips, and in my haste to cover my loud mouth, I fumbled my phone. Knowing the likelihood of it surviving a fall into the rocks was low, even in the protective case, my hands flailed to avoid dropping it, which threw my balance off.

I never did quite pinpoint what ran out of the woods.

Because once my balance faltered, so did I, and the next thing I knew, my legs were tangled underneath me, snagging in the hanging ends of my poncho. The slick fabric became almost slimy in the water, making my attempt to stand up, to move away from the stream, futile.

Any concern I had for my phone was quickly replaced with concern for my life as my hands clawed at the rocks, attempting a grip that wouldn't happen. Underneath me, the poncho was acting like a lubricant, sliding easily over the water-worn stones, easing me toward the mountainside.

And then... off it.

"Well, it's about time, Sleeping Beauty."

Those words were tinged with amusement, and even though I didn't recognize the voice, it was soothing and earnest, so I smiled.

Well... more like a cringe, due to the explosion of pain that happened when I tried to curve my lips that way.

"*Goddamnit*," I hissed, my eyes still partially closed as I lifted a hand, searching for the source of the pain. Warm fingers covered mine, stopping me as I contacted the coarse gauze of a bandage.

"Don't you go messing up Doc's work now," the voice scolded, even as she offered the motherly comfort of a pat on my hand as she pressed it back to my side. "You're alright."

I believed her.

With a voice like that, like warm peach cobbler, why the hell wouldn't I?

"I... I can't *see*," I pleaded, not understanding why. There was a vague strip of light, but outside of that, it was like I couldn't open my eyes.

"Wouldn't make much sense if you could." Something shifted, and my eyelids felt lighter. Finally, I was able to pull them open, only to immediately squint against the light. "See there? We were trying to protect you from that."

Disregarding the pain – and the scolding – I forced my eyes open, willing the image in front of me to come into focus. A blurry silhouette hovered over me, vaguely woman-shaped, with no discernible features save for a generous streak of gray at the front of her head. I blinked once, and that helped, allowing me to make out a smile to match the nurturing reassurance of her voice.

"Where am I?" I rasped, tentatively casting my gaze around me at the wood-paneled walls. There was a sizeable window across the room, and even with the paisley-printed curtains drawn, sunbeams still spilled through.

"After a fall like that? Doc's office, honey."

I frowned, forcing my energy toward sorting through the fog in my brain.

That's right.

I fell.

That sudden recollection put me on high alert, but my attempt to sit up was immediately thwarted, with a firm hand inhibiting me from rising more than a couple of inches from the bed.

"Whoa now," the woman said, wagging a finger at me. "I'll help you sit up if that's what you want to do, but you've gotta take it slow. You hit your head pretty good, so we gotta be careful."

Now *that* part, I didn't remember at all. Almost dropping the phone, then slipping, sliding off the edge of the mountain – those were all clear in my mind. Anything between that and waking up in this room?

It wasn't even fuzzy.

It just wasn't there at all.

I accepted the help she'd offered to sit up, using the opportunity to acquaint myself with features that were growing clearer. She had coarse dark hair – except that streak of gray - pulled into a neatly shaped bun, and skin the same warm amber tone as honey, stippled with slightly darker freckles.

"You're the doctor?" I asked, eliciting a laugh from her.

"No honey, that's Lilah. I'm Regina Wilburn."

My eyes narrowed. "As in... Wilburn Rentals?"

Her grin deepened, bringing up twin dimples. "Yes ma'am. I'm sitting in for Dr. Atwood until she gets back from riding with Deena Aldridge up to the hospital with the twins. All the serious stuff gets sent up to the city."

"Falling off the side of a mountain... *isn't* serious?"

Regina scoffed. "Around here? Who *hasn't* taken a lil' tumble off Big Sugar? That's what *we* call it, you know?"

"I do now," I agreed, with a slight nod that only made the pain in my head worse. "And you said you're... *not* a doctor?"

"No, but I can holler down the hall for Nurse Ellis if you need me to. I'm here to make sure your monitors don't stop pinging."

That wasn't *too* surprising.

Sugar Valley was a charming small town, tucked neatly into the dense maple forest that started at the base of Sugar Leaf mountain – *Big Sugar*, as the locals apparently called it. On the drive in, I'd admired the old-school "main street". Ornamental maples lining the footpaths, striped canopies, hanging flower pots on the light posts, and hand-painted signs in the storefronts.

Nostalgia was *not* in short supply in Sugar Valley but trained medical staff... *was*.

"I'm fine, I think," I told Regina, not wanting her to trouble the already limited staff on my account. Now that I was vertical, and my vision wasn't quite as hazy, I felt more lucid. Unfortunately, clarity brought pain.

And so did my reflection in the mirror.

The seconds *before* I saw myself hurt a lot less than the seconds *after*. Something about *seeing* the nicks and bruises that marred my face and arms – and the rest of me too, I could feel but not see, underneath the sheets – seemed to make them smart a little more. And judging from the size of the bandage, I didn't even want to see what *"hitting my head pretty good"* looked like. It *felt* bad enough.

"You definitely are, Dr. Atwood said so. She checked you out before she left. You can even go on to your lodge if you'd like – your orders are to rest up and keep your bandages clean. Ben found you out on the ridge. You got lucky – tree branches caught you, kept you up. He said he had to untangle you from your rain gear."

I sighed.

So many names, not enough faces.

"And who is Ben? Where is Ben?"

Regina sucked her teeth. "Ain't no telling what he's off doing, or where he is."

"Okay. I... just wanted to say thank you, I guess. For not leaving me out there for the... what kind of animals are in these woods?"

"Black bears and coyotes, honey."

My eyes widened. "Oh. Yes. Those. Thank him for not leaving me out there... with those. Where might I find him?"

Regina smirked, amused by some inside joke I wasn't privy

to, at least not yet. "I wouldn't worry about it if I were you, but I'm sure you'll see him around."

Well, that's not curiosity-inspiring at all...

"Oh. Okay, um... thank you."

"You're welcome," she told me, granting a bright smile. "And your room is ready when you're ready."

"My room?"

She nodded. "Your lodge, remember? It's ready now. Sorry about that mix up earlier – my nephew should've put a discount on your bill."

"Oh! Yes, he was lovely. But um... all my bags are in the car I rented, still at the base of the mountain."

She waved off my concern. "Your keys and everything else that was in your pockets is right there on the bedside table. Ben drove you into town in your car. It's in the parking lot, but I hope you'll let me drive you since I'm going back over there anyway."

I'd never met this woman before today, but it somehow struck me as ridiculous to argue against it. I'd knocked myself out falling off the side of a mountain on the *first* day – hell, within the first few hours – of what was supposed to be an escape.

Surely, I could trust the woman whose property I'd be staying on for the next... however long... to drive me "home".

"I'd appreciate that," I told her, which seemed to make her happy. Her shoulders perked immediately, and she started moving around, gathering my things into a plain plastic bag. "There wouldn't happen to be a cell phone among all that, would there?" I asked, already suspecting the answer but hoping I was wrong.

Regina shook her head. "These are the only things he brought in, but perhaps he left some things in your car?"

"Maybe…"

A long, low sigh pushed from my throat as my eyes landed on the simple analog clock that hung over the door. Assuming it was right, it was nearly evening – hours after I first set foot in Sugar Valley.

Hours after the time I'd agreed to call my mother.

Cookie Desmond had been firmly, decidedly, utterly *against* her oldest daughter – me – *"going all Naked and Afraid"* as she'd tearfully referred to my decision to spend my self-imposed sabbatical in Sugar Valley. No number of forwarded articles convinced her that this town was nobody's backwoods Tennessee, or some horror movie setup. I understood her fears – even had a few myself – but ultimately, I'd decided that this was it.

This place would be a desperately needed respite before I…

Before you what?

I shook my head.

My first day here had gotten off to a rough enough start. I had *plenty* of time to obsess about my emotional state – or lack thereof. For now, I *needed* to call Cookie before that woman called up the troops – my siblings, and her siblings, and my father's siblings, and whoever else she could recruit to descend on Sugar Valley looking for me.

Requesting a phone to call my mother only deepened Regina's dimples, and she handed me her own, stepping out of the room to give me privacy. I swung my legs out of bed, grimacing at the cuts and bruises that covered them.

Wonderful.

Rolling my eyes, I tapped in the number to my parents' house – the same number it had been since I was a little girl, giggling into it for hours with my friends. While it rang, I gingerly stood, testing to make sure I wasn't dealing with any sort of sprain or tweak before I took the steps to cross the room for the window.

"*Desmond residence, you're speaking to Dean.*"

My father's deep, rumbling tenor brought an instant smile to my face, like always.

"Daddy, hey," I told him, suddenly wishing I'd asked for a glass of water or something to soothe my dry throat. There had never been a moment in my life that my father hadn't seen straight through any attempt to downplay my pain, emotional or otherwise.

Sounding like I'd swallowed glass certainly wouldn't help.

"Doodle?!"

"*Oh God,*" I groaned, rolling my eyes at the corny, cutesy nickname I not-so-secretly loved. "Really dude?"

He chuckled. "Til the day you or I die, whichever one comes first... maybe you, once your mother gets ahold of you."

"What did *I* do?"

"You didn't call her when you were supposed to, and ain't answering that damn cell phone. You know how she gets."

I sighed. "I do. Is she there?"

"She's around here somewhere, stomping around downstairs, fussing about you to one of your aunts. You want me to get her?"

"*No!*" I couldn't get *that* out fast enough. "Just tell her I called, and that I um... I lost my phone. I'll work on finding it tomorrow, but I'm fine. I'm okay."

Thick silence stretched over the phone, filling out enough space to make me uncomfortable before my father rumbled, "Are you *really?*"

Shit.

"Yes. I... had a little spill on my hike. But the doctor checked me out, and I'm fine."

"Little girl..."

"I'm thirty-six!"

"Don't mean shit to me," he laughed, slapping away my attempt to assert myself as a fully grown adult. "But if you say you're good, I'll let you be... and put a leash on your mama. For now. *Call her tomorrow*."

Even though he couldn't see me, I nodded. "I will. I promise."

"Okay baby. Love you."

"I love you too, Daddy. Bye."

I let go of the breath I'd been holding as we ended the call, knowing that I'd only narrowly dodged a bullet that would be coming back for me the next day. Still, a hot bath tonight and a good breakfast in the morning would go a long way to bringing me into a better headspace for that unavoidable conversation.

Pushing the curtain aside, I peeked out the window to see that the "Doc's office" was part of the Main Street I'd admired on my way into town. I'd have significantly fewer bumps and bruises if I'd simply spent my time exploring Sugar Valley while I waited for my room to be ready, instead of venturing up the mountain.

A knock at the door drew my attention away from the window, and a moment later, Regina peeked inside.

"I just thought about it – do you want me to bring one of your bags, so you can change clothes?"

Heat rushed to my face as I glanced down, registering for the first time that I was in my bra, tank top, and boy short panties – the things I'd worn underneath my hiking clothes this morning. Not entirely naked, but not the first impression I wanted to make on the town.

"Yes, please. I would appreciate that very much," I told her, taking the opportunity to return her phone as well. "Thank you for letting me use this."

"No problem at all. I'll be right back with your bag."

Regina stepped out again, and I dropped into a seat on the bed, just as my stomach growled. I hadn't eaten since the early morning hours, an issue that would have to be rectified sooner than later, along with finding my phone.

Tracking down this "Ben" would probably be a good start.

I couldn't sleep.

I wished I could blame it on my head, or one of the other bumps and bruises I'd attained in my "tumble" off the side of Big Sugar, but this was... something else.

Something I'd battled with before I'd ever even arrived in Sugar Valley.

Bright orange flames licked at the heavy logs in the fireplace, crackling and popping as they transformed wood to ash. For what felt like hours, I'd been trying to lose myself in the hypnotic dance of the fire, but my brain insisted on remaining firmly rooted in my present state of... *emptiness*.

But now that everything else had been stripped away, what did I expect?

I let out a huff, then grabbed the fireplace poker, spreading the woods and ashes into a flat pile. From there, I picked up the little shovel, using it to move ashes from the bottom of the fireplace over the current fire, doing that until it was submerged, as I'd been instructed.

Then I got up.

In the bathroom, I unbraided my hair from the two plaits it had been in all day, using the length to mask the bandage that was still covering the – uglier than expected – gash on the side of my head. Regina had left out the fact that I'd needed a few stitches, but that didn't matter now. What mattered was *Maple*, the restaurant with the after-hours bar up at the main lodge which she *had* told me about.

I needed a damn drink.

After doing the best I could with my hair, I used my makeup bag to cover the cuts and bruises on my face, then dressed in leggings and a light, oversized sweater. Up in these mountains, the temperature drop at night was drastic, which worked in my favor. I didn't care, not even a little, about being cute – I just wasn't in the mood for questions.

I tucked my lodge key into a tiny cross body bag I'd brought along for times like this when all I needed was my absolute essentials. Unfortunately, my phone was still somewhere up on that mountain, for now. It would just be lip balm, wallet and keys tonight.

A slight shiver ran up my spine as I stepped out of my cabin, into a temperature that was a little lower than I expected. Briefly, I contemplated dipping back inside for warmer clothes but quickly changed my mind.

It felt good to *feel* something.

Anything.

The lodges were set apart from the actual town, by a single road that couldn't have run more than two or three miles before you reached one or the other. The road dipped down into the "valley" where the founders of this area had broken ground, making the town look even further away. From where I stood, on the porch of my cabin, Sugar Valley looked like a village of miniatures, with those charming streetlights making Main Street glow.

I closed my eyes, blocking that view before it elicited unwelcome memories. Instead, I focused my attention on the property I was already on, focusing my gaze on the biggest of the lodges, grinning at the glowing neon maple leaf affixed to the front. My mouth was already watering as I headed in that direction.

Inside, I wasn't surprised to find it mostly empty. It was nearly one in the morning, and all the other tourists were asleep, leaving *Maple* to me, a guy tucked to himself at the end of the bar, the bartender, and a lone server who was too engrossed in her cell phone to even look up when I walked in.

But that was fine.

I wasn't concerned about the service, not at this time of night. I crossed the polished hardwood floor, admiring the exposed beams and modern lighting and décor before I took a seat at the bar.

"What are you drinking, gorgeous?" the bartender asked, leaning much further over the bar top than he needed to, to make sure I understood that his attention was on me. He was handsome – *very* handsome, actually – but there was, very clearly, a wedding band on his finger. Not that it mattered, since I wasn't here – in the bar, or on this mountain – for that anyway, but still... I noticed.

"I heard that there was a distillery around here..." I started, propping my elbow on the bar, chin in my hand. "You know anything about that?"

My question brought an instant grin to his lips. "Of course I know something about that. Home-grown bourbon aged in home-grown maple barrels. You want it straight up?"

"God no," I chuckled, shaking my head. "An Old-Fashioned. And a slice of the maple pecan pie I heard about if the kitchen isn't..." I glanced over my shoulder at the server, who still hadn't looked up from her phone. "Too busy."

"Old-Fashioned and pecan pie, coming right up," he assured.

Moments later, I had my drink and my dessert, and the

bartender moved to the other end of the bar to flirt with the server, who had attention to spare for *him*.

Again though, that was fine, because I had what I needed – a stiff cocktail and a decadent dessert. I could do without the attention or the conversation. Solace gave me the chance to get lost in—

"Careful not to overdo it... wouldn't want you taking another spill."

The smooth whiskey turned to acid in my throat as I choked on it, then coughed to clear the suddenly offensive liquid from my airway. My gaze shot upward, searching for the source of that casually leveled taunt, landing at the end of the bar opposite the hushed flirting.

There was only one person there.

"Excuse me?" I asked, certain that I had to have misheard his statement. There were five seats, a turn, and another five seats between us, so it was feasible that—

"*Make sure you can get yourself home,*" he repeated, with no less derision than before, and leaning in this time to make sure I heard. The shift in position pulled him out of the shadows, bringing the soft illumination of the bar onto dark skin and sculpted features. "Don't want to have to rescue you again."

Again...?

My eyes narrowed as I quickly put together the clues.

"I'm guessing you're... Ben?"

The slight downturn of his lips reversed, switching into a mocking smirk. "In the flesh. You're welcome."

My face twisted, one eyebrow up, the other down. "Uh... Thank you?"

"Didn't save your ass for *you*," he jeered, lifting the glass with his chosen poison, draining the rest with one gulp. "Those animals out there taste human flesh, you ruin it for everybody. Should've thought about that before you decided to go traipsing around on the mountain for Instagram. This shit is real, sweetheart. No filter."

"*Kiss my ass*" was right on the tip of my tongue, but I held it, clenching my jaw tight. "I am *well* aware that the mountain is real, and I'm not here for a photo op, but thanks for the tip."

"My bad. You have a *sponsored* look about you."

"And what the hell is *that* supposed to mean?" I snapped, giving up on the idea of biting my tongue – I'd had enough pain for one night.

"Luxury rental, designer luggage, diamond studs in your ears to go hiking..."

"I wear earrings *everywhere*," I defended, reflexively bringing a defensive hand to my ear. "And I paid for everything I have my damn self – *not* that it's your business."

He scoffed, propping his elbows on the bar top. The light gray thermal he wore pulled at his thick biceps as he leaned in. "See, that's where you're wrong, because *you* made it my business when your bougie ass fell off the mountain, and *I* had to save you. The straps on your little designer backpack damn near killed you, by the way."

"And where might I *find* my backpack, by the way?" I stabbed at my pecan pie with more force than necessary, breaking off another piece to shove into my mouth in hopes that the sweetness would help calm my building rage. "And my phone."

"Hell if I know," he shrugged, sounding vaguely pleased by his unhelpful answer. "I didn't even see a phone, and I wasn't about to argue with the bear who was getting ready to drag you off because of whatever the hell you had in the bag that it smelled and wanted. I just cut the straps off you, so it could go on its way. Again – *you're welcome*."

"And I've already said *thank you*," I reminded him, lip curled. "What more do you want me to do?"

"I want you to not feed the bears junk food or drop electronics to corrode the ecosystem of the woods, or roll around disrupting root systems and shit."

I rolled my eyes. "Wow. Next time I'll be sure to keep my near-death experience a little more contained. I am *so sorry*."

He smirked. "Apology accepted. And yes, your attention to your impact on the forest moving forward would be *greatly* appreciated."

"What the hell is your problem?" I asked, finishing off my own drink to calm my suddenly frazzled nerves.

He stood, taking up way more vertical space than I expected before he ambled around the corner of the bar, hands shoved into the pockets of low-slung jeans. The smirk he'd been wearing graduated into a smile – the kind of smile that, even though it was snide, was also a bit... flutter-inducing. Which was a bit... *crazy*.

"My *problem*," he drawled, stopping just outside of too close, but still close enough that I smelled him – whiskey and laundry detergent and outdoors. "Is tourists who come up here with no experience and no respect, tearing shit up and then leaving, with no regard for anybody but themselves."

My fingers flexed around my cold, empty glass, nostrils flared. "You don't even *know* me."

Ben's head tilted, lips twisted in contempt. "You say that as if it's a problem."

My mouth opened, but nothing came out, and he left me like that, looking stupid, forced to deal with the low-level rage he'd induced all on my own. I let out a huff, then turned back to my pie with my heart racing, suddenly understanding why Regina had – vaguely – warned me not to bother with thanking him for getting me out of the woods.

Apparently, Ben was a *known* asshole.

Shaking my head, I stuffed another forkful of pie into my

mouth, savoring the sweetness as I waited for my heart to stop racing, and for the adrenaline to let down. After an encounter like that, all I wanted to do was crawl into the big king-sized bed at the lodge and sleep it off.

With any luck... tomorrow would be better.

CHAPTER TWO

I could sit out here for hours.

Camouflaged among the leaves, watching.

Not the people – the people were boring as hell, always as predictably annoying as I expected. They never held my attention unless they were destroying something, which was... painfully often. Sometimes I intervened, quelling the potential damage of a picnic full of trash left behind in an undesignated area, or some thrill-seeking teenagers thinking a picture of them hanging off the falls would be the thing that made them go viral. Other times, I let the consequences happen – like hornet stings after venturing into an area where they'd been notified with clearly marked signs not to go.

Either way, I found myself playing clean-up so consistently that I could time it to a clock, and spent the moments after counting down until I didn't have to. To when I could settle into my surroundings and observe what I wanted.

Anything else.

Everything else.

From my perch on the mountain, I watched.

A majestic black bear washing itself in the cool comfort of a natural pool. Hundreds of yards away, a small pack of deer grazing through the sugar maple saplings near the west base of the mountain, and...

A poncho-covered tourist, heading up the trail to the first viewing area for the falls, even though the trail was closed today, due to the weather forecast.

Goddamnit.

My grip around my binoculars tightened as I watched this idiot slip and slide in the slick moisture left behind by the thunderstorms that had swept over the mountain earlier. The forecast called for more, scattered throughout the day, bringing the kind of thunder and lightning and natural destruction that *would've* made for a perfect day with a fresh bottle of bourbon.

Drinking and watching.

Instead, I had to get this dumbass off the mountain before they got hurt.

I extricated myself from my place in the trees near my house, crossing the distance with a quick jog to my front porch, where I kept a bag of gear waiting. I strapped it on, then brought my binoculars back to my face to pinpoint exactly where this nitwit was and calculate where they might be by the time I made it down.

From my slightly different vantage point now, I saw them better – well enough to make out a detail that made my eyes narrow.

I *recognized* the purple accent on those hiking boots.

"*No way she's this goddamn stupid,*" I muttered to myself, looking even harder now, hoping that the woman from yesterday was *not* quite that stupid. The person rounded a ridge, and I caught a glimpse of skin – the same deep, coppery gold that had caught my attention the day before, tangled in a different poncho from the one she wore now.

Rescuing her then hadn't even required a second thought.

Immediately after I saw *her*, I'd seen the bear pawing at the designer backpack that was tangled around her arm, presumably after something he'd smelled coming from it, picking up the difference between that and the typical scents of the woods.

She wasn't supposed to be down there. There was no trail, no place to make a smooth descent, so she had to have fallen. Bears – at least the ones in these woods – weren't natural human predators. The females, especially, had a very *don't start no shit, won't be none* approach to humans, so merely not provoking them was usually enough. Whatever the woman had in her bag though... it changed things a little. The presence of food – food that it *wanted* – made bear behavior less predictable. It was an easy choice to pull out my knife, cut those straps off her, and let the bear go on its way with the bag.

Most people, after an incident like that – conscious or not – would avoid putting themselves in the same position. But as she pulled the hood of her poncho off, stopping for a moment to wipe moisture from her face, giving me a clear view in the process, I realized... this woman was *not* most people.

And not in a good way.

I headed down the mountain to where she was, only stopping along the way to curse and put on my own rain gear as the rain started up again, in a steady drizzle that made the trail even more dangerous. Last night's storm had altered the terrain – another reason the path was closed. I hadn't cleared away the branches ripped down by the wind, tested the trees for lightning damage, sprinkled the gravel that would turn slick patches into areas that the soles of your shoes could grip.

It pissed me off, more than a little, that this woman had blatantly ignored the signs that the trail was closed – she quite literally had to climb over the chain I'd latched across the forest entrance myself in the early hours of the morning. Not only was she putting herself in danger, but now *I* was risking twisted ankles and enduring the discomfort of getting rained on to save her ass from herself.

When I ran into her last night, I'd held back.

This time, I wouldn't.

I caught up with her just before the last ridge before she would reach the first viewing area, which was where she'd fallen from the day before.

"*Hey!*" I called, getting her attention as her foot landed on the first of the natural steps that time and weather had carved into the side of the mountain. "What the hell do you think you're doing?"

Her eyes were wide when she turned around, but she made no move to step down. Instead, she gestured behind her. "I'm hiking."

"The trail is closed. I'm assuming you can't read, but that's what that big ass sign down at the bottom, attached to that chain meant."

Her nostrils flared, top lip curled into a sneer. "Yeah, I caught that. But I'm looking for something I dropped yesterday. I need to find it, and then I'll be right back down."

"No." I stepped toward her, face set into a glare that she couldn't possibly mistake for friendly, using a tone she couldn't possibly mistake as negotiable. "You're going to take your ass back down this mountain right now. Whatever you need to look for, it can wait."

She crossed her arms, lips pursed in defiance. "Says *who*?"

"Says *me*."

"On what authority?"

I didn't have to go back and forth with this woman – loathed the idea of it. But to prove my point – and hopefully get her ass moving faster – I pulled up the front of my poncho, showing her the uniform I wore, and the name badge affixed to it.

Her scowl deepened. "Park ranger, huh?"

"Forest," I corrected.

"You armed?"

I raised an eyebrow. "Yes. I am."

For most normal people, the asking and answering of that question would have prompted cooperation, for fear of getting shot. Her gaze dropped, to where I did indeed have a handgun holstered to my side, then back up to my face as she lowered her arms from the defiant stance she'd been in.

And then she turned and ran up those goddamn steps.

Because she was not most people.

"*Shit*," I muttered under my breath as she slipped out of view over that ridge. Part of me wanted to leave her to her fate, but I had a responsibility to fulfill, a sense of duty that wouldn't allow me to walk away.

Especially after the rolling boom of thunder that sounded a few seconds later, and the bright crack of lightning that lit the sky barely a minute after. Already, the usual blue was tinged light gray, and darker clouds were rolling in fast. I took the steps behind her as safely as I could, and found her with her head bowed, eyes on the ground as she moved near the cliff.

In front of us, water gushed down the falls, bolstered by the earlier rainfall. Slicker conditions and a faster current made this area, usually not dangerous at all, a reasonably hazardous place to be. It had been slippery yesterday, sure, but the chances of an accident were exponentially higher in weather like this.

We needed to get off this mountain, *now*.

I didn't even say anything, I simply hooked an arm around her waist, easily pulling her with me.

"*Waiiit!*" she screamed. "I just saw it! Put me down!"

"Whatever it is, it can wait," I growled, unmoved by her pleas. I was, however, moved by a well-placed kick to the shin, the blow startling me enough that she managed to wriggle free. Before I caught her, she darted away, slipping and falling hard enough that it *had* to hurt, but she kept moving, crawling to snatch up what I realized was a cell phone.

A soaking wet cell phone.

"*Bring your ass*," I bellowed at her, snatching her up from the ground in tandem with another boom of thunder. This time, the accompanying flash of lightning came even faster. Keeping a grip on her arm, I ignored her attempts to pull away, and bristled at her objections as I pulled her down off that ridge, and then back the way I'd come through the forest.

"This is the wrong way!" she shouted, over the cacophony of noise that bloomed around us as the storm hit, each large, harsh raindrop making a different sound as it connected with the various textures of the forest. I paid her no mind though, intent on making it to my destination through a landscape I was well-acquainted with.

As relieved as I was to reach the familiar clearing, I didn't let that slow my steps *or* hers, practically dragging her up my front porch as the storm hit. Even there, under the protection of the wide awning, rain whipped at us from what seemed like all sides until I got the front door unlocked, and pulled us in.

The woman – *Kyle*, according to the ID I'd found in her pocket the day before – stood at the front window, catching her breath for a moment before she seemed to remember the cell phone in her hand. The smile that spread over her face was one of such deep relief that it stunned me for a second.

It's just a damn smartphone...

One she could've replaced right in Sugar Valley, in less time, with a lot less hassle, than the stunt she'd pulled. I had no idea what could've been so important about that goddamn phone, but I did know one thing – there was no way I was about to let her enjoy this little happy ending as easily as she thought.

I strode up to her, pulling the device from her hands while she was still staring at it like a lost treasure. The sudden absence made the color drain from her face, and her eyes were wide when she immediately moved to snatch it back.

"Give that to me, *now*," she hissed, with enough venom that it made me lift an eyebrow.

"Not until you tell me what the hell you were thinking, going up the mountain in this weather. This is *exactly* what I was talking about last night."

She growled, adding to her collection of frustrated animal noises as she tried in vain to tug down my arm. "I was *thinking* that I needed my phone and that I should get it before it got washed away forever."

"So you risk your life and mine for some circuits and glass?"

"Nobody was thinking about you!" She stepped back, her gaze darting around, looking for something unknown. Until her gaze landed on the collection of hiking poles by the door and lit up, and then I *knew* very well.

"Hey!" I bellowed, moving in front of her. "Don't even think about it. Did you forget I told your ass I was armed?!"

She shrugged, tossing up her hands. "So shoot me! And then give me back my *goddamn phone!*"

For a second, I thought I might *have* to, when she launched herself at me, fists flying toward my face. I dropped the phone to catch her by the wrists, stopping her attempted assault long enough to pin her wrists together between us.

"Have you lost your damn mind?"

The roar of my voice seemed to snap her out of that sudden rage. When she noticed both of my hands occupied with keeping her from going Tori McNab on me, her eyes widened, searching the ground for the phone I'd let drop.

She tried to pull away, but I held her firm as yet another roar of thunder shook the house. The harder she tugged, the tighter I gripped, until her gaze lifted to meet mine, desperate and pleading.

"*Please*," she whimpered, and then... *deflated*. All her rage and bravado melted away – she just wanted to get to that phone.

So I let her.

I released her from my hold, and she immediately dove for the phone, scrambling away from me once she had it in her hands. Seeing the way she held it to her chest, I wasn't even interested in harassing her about it anymore.

Domino's entrance drew my attention away from Kyle. She was notoriously sleepy whenever it rained and had spent the morning snoozing in her dog bed, basking in the residual warmth from the fireplace. Now, presumably, the commotion had woken her up, and she was coming to investigate. She eyed Kyle, probably wondering who the hell she was, then came to me, pushing her head under my hand for reassurance.

"C'mon girl," I muttered, leading her toward the kitchen, where I poured out some dry food and refilled her water bowl. After I had Dom settled, I started a new fire and then changed into dry clothes before I headed back to the foyer to look in on Kyle, hoping that some time alone had calmed her ass down.

I found her with her poncho – and *pants* – off, digging through the new-looking backpack she'd been wearing under her rain gear. Instead of moving closer, I cleared my throat, which startled her enough to go scrambling backward before she fell on her ass, a can of bear spray in one hand, and a first aid kit in the other.

"Don't come near me," she warned, brandishing that bear spray, which I scoffed at. I didn't *want* to go near her, but my gaze scanned her bare legs, still covered in yesterdays cuts and scrapes, plus a new injury – a badly scraped knee that had her bleeding all over the hardwood floor I'd laid myself.

"That needs a real washing," I told her, as casually as possible, trying my best not to sound like I gave a damn. I didn't know if she was truly afraid, or just cold, but she was trembling, sitting there in her panties and a soaked tee shirt, and her thick hair sending rivulets of water down her face. "And you probably need the bandage on your head replaced too."

I saw the realization cross her face – wide eyes, parted lips, and then a quick shuttering of her expression like she didn't want me to see. Her shoulders dropped, and so did the bear spray, her chest heaving as she blew out a sigh.

"So now you see how idiotic it was to go up that mountain after a goddamn phone?"

Her head popped up again, eyes full of fire as she wiped the water from her face. "What turned you into such a mean sonofabitch, huh?"

Smirking, I walked up to her, easily hefting her from the ground and taking that bear spray, which I tossed back into her open bag. "Life."

She sighed again but said nothing as I took her into the kitchen, depositing her on the counter near the sink. I pulled out my first aid kit – a *real* first aid kit – putting it down beside her before I motioned for her to put her feet in the sink.

"*Shit*," she hissed under her breath, flinching as I used the spray nozzle to wash away the dirt and blood from her skin. Just as I'd been trained for, I clean, dried, and dressed the wound, which was bad enough that she would've had trouble doing it for herself.

Once that was taken care of, I addressed the bandage on her head, covering the gash she'd acquired in yesterday's fall. She used an elastic band from her wrist to contain her hair, giving me room to change out the rain-soaked dressing for a new, dry one.

"Thank you," she said after it was done, and I was packing the first aid kit away. The fire had been going long enough to warm the house, so she wasn't trembling as much anymore.

Still... with her legs hanging off the counter, bandaged head, bandaged leg... she looked pitiful.

"Just doing what I'm supposed to," I told her, even though that was... a bit of an exaggeration. Leaving her out there in the elements would've been a dereliction of duty, but everything else, I probably could've gotten away with not doing.

She looked up, pinning me with big brown eyes that were harder to look away from than I was comfortable with. "People don't do what they're supposed to all the time. So like I said... thank you."

"Whatever. Just keep your ass off the mountain when it's closed." I bent to stow the first aid kit back in its place under the sink. "Or... period. That would work for me too."

Her lips curved up into a smirk. "Hate to disappoint you, but I'll be around for a while, and I have every intention of becoming familiar with this mountain."

"You'd better superglue that damned phone to your hand then, or your silly ass will fall off again, looking for it."

Mentioning the phone killed that smirk. She looked away from me, focusing on a random place on the wall.

"You know you could've gotten a new one down in town, right?"

She blinked, then shook her head. "No. This one can't be replaced."

My eyebrows pulled together. "What's so damn special about it?"

At first, she didn't answer. She just... *stared*. But then a tiny stream of water broke through the coiled edges of her hair, dripping onto her face, and she shook her head again. "I don't think you'd understand."

My brow loosened. "Yeah. You're probably right."

With that, she pushed herself down from the counter, brushing past me to head back toward the foyer. Reflexively, my gaze dropped, to where the bottoms of her ass cheeks were peeking beneath the line of the bright yellow panties she wore. Somehow, she must've felt it, because she looked back with a scowl, tugging the back of her shirt down as she kept walking.

"You need some dry clothes?" I called after her, with no attempt to keep my laughter at bay.

"I have what I need," she snapped, stopping in the hallway to turn to me. "A change of clothes in my bag. As soon as the storm passes, I'll be out of your way. Hopefully, sooner than later."

"Your lips to God's ears."

That earned me a roll of her eyes, and she stomped on back to the foyer, leaving me with the sweet lingering scent of whatever perfume she wore.

"Who the fuck wears perfume in the mountains?" I muttered to Domino, who'd approached me again with questioning eyes that I had no answers for. She wasn't used to me having strange people here and was undoubtedly ready for Kyle to leave.

Meaning we were all on the same page.

CHAPTER THREE

The rain wouldn't stop.

In fact, it almost seemed like the longer I stared out the window, the worse it got, every crash of thunder and streak of lightning an admonition that the storm would pass when it *wanted* to, and not a moment sooner.

Whenever it ended, it wouldn't be soon enough.

I needed to get the hell out of here.

The fact that I was trapped in a house with a stranger was terrible enough – once I factored in that he was a flat-out jerk, my situation was far from pretty. Finding peace had been my primary reason for this whole trip, and right now, I was *far* from that.

Unsettled.

Annoyed.

Starving.

Ugh.

Recognizing the hunger clawing at the inside of my belly only seemed to make it worse, and now I was kicking myself for not sticking a few snacks in my bag. I knew better, but I'd had Ben's voice in my head while I was packing my backpack – his reprimand from the night before, about the effects of the pre-packaged food on the wildlife in the forest.

Of course I didn't *plan* to have my bag ravaged by wild animals, but that *just-in-case* feeling had gnawed at me until I rationalized that I wouldn't be on the mountain long anyway.

Without even trying, he'd made a fool of me again, but I certainly didn't have to give him the satisfaction of knowing. My water bottle was still full, and I had a whole tin of mints. Surely it couldn't storm *too* much longer... right?

That thought had barely gotten across my mind before another roll of thunder cracked the sky as if the weather were answering my question with a loud, "Try me, bitch."

The lightning was the exclamation mark.

"You know you can't will away a storm, right?"

My eyes narrowed.

Just the sound of his voice put me on edge.

Reluctantly, I turned to see Ben resting against the wall on the other side of the room, hands tucked into the pockets of the sweats he'd donned after changing from his wet clothes earlier.

"Everything is impossible, until somebody does it for the first time," I countered, crossing my arms.

"And a watched pot never boils, if throwing out bullshit quotables is what we're doing right now."

"You can kiss my ass if being a jerk is what *you're* doing right now."

That brought a smirk to his lips as he lifted his hands. "I'll pass on the ass-kissing. I was coming to ask if you were hungry. We've been here a while."

Hmph.

That was an understatement. We'd been here long enough that I'd watched the sky fade from gray to black, with the occasional strike of lightning offering the only illumination.

"I'm fine," I answered, while my stomach sounded off a loud

protest of its empty state, sending fresh heat to my cheeks as Ben chuckled, not even doing me the courtesy of looking away.

He looked me right in the eyes, perfectly happy to *not* hide that he found my discomfort humorous.

"You can't starve in my house," he said, very matter-of-fact. "You've caused me enough grief – Your malnutrition isn't a problem I need."

"Fine. If you have a granola bar or something, I—"

"I made you a sandwich when I made mine. Tell me you don't have any food allergies, or sensitivities, or any of that shit," he said, in a tone that suggested he thought of those things as character flaws, rather than medical conditions.

"I don't."

"Good. Come eat."

I hated myself for following his rude-ass command, but I followed him into the kitchen, where I saw two plates at the counter. Seeing them next to each other surprised me – I *never* would have thought he'd want us to eat together. That was quickly killed though, when he grabbed his plate and took it to the other end of the kitchen, putting his attention on his laptop and mostly ignoring me.

Whatever.

Instead of dwelling on his frostiness toward me, I focused on the sandwich, which I was grateful for. Maybe I was just hungry as hell, but it felt like the best sandwich I'd ever eaten, even though it was just turkey and gouda, with some type of spicy mayo. I devoured it – and the kettle-cooked chips on the side – in what had to be record timing, then swallowed the bottle of water he'd left there for me too.

I didn't look up until everything was gone, and when I did, I found Ben staring at me, his expression a combination of confusion, fascination, and... a little low level repulsion.

"I've never seen anybody eat that fast. *Dom* doesn't even eat that fast," he said, pointing toward the fluffy black-and-white dog that had been side-eyeing me since I came through the door. "Maybe you *would've* been good out there in the wilderness on your own."

I took a deep breath, swallowing my offense, since he was trying to get under my skin, for whatever reason. His problem – his *real* problem – had nothing to do with me.

He was just an asshole.

"Thank you for the food," I told him, carefully measuring my tone as I spoke. I'd already had to give up the *don't let him know I'm hungry* point. He wasn't about to get this one too.

He shrugged, chomping on a mouthful himself.

His sandwich was only half gone.

Damn, am I greedy like that?

"I – correctly, obviously – assumed you wouldn't be properly prepared for a trip up the mountain, so like I said... I couldn't let you starve."

"Why are you such an asshole?" I snapped, his latest insult driving away any impulse I had to save face. "I thought it was just your nature, but it seems like you have a problem with me, specifically."

"I had to drag your ass inside from a storm because you thought it was a good idea to come up here chasing a damn cell phone, and you have to *ask* what my problem with you is? You're not very perceptive, are you?"

"It's not even *about* the goddamn phone!"

"Then what *is* it about?!"

"You don't deserve to know," I hissed, jabbing a finger in his direction. "It'll be a cold day in hell before I use my personal shit to justify myself to an arrogant prick like you."

Again, he shrugged. "I don't care anyway, so that's no problem."

For the second time, I stomped off, back to the little space

I'd created for myself in his foyer. Just like before, I was steaming mad, and just like before, I picked up the controversial cell phone.

I'd been so, *so* relieved earlier to discover that it was still working.

Of course, that part was secondary to possession of the device itself, but that didn't mean plugging it into my portable charger and seeing it power on hadn't been a relief too. I ran my fingers over the embossed edges of the hot pink and electric purple protective shell, letting a smile creep to my face. Neither of those was exactly my favorite color, but the case had done its job. And besides that, it had been a gift – a gift I'd promised to treasure.

I'd die before I broke that promise.

I clapped a hand over my mouth to stifle my surprised shriek when the phone started ringing, unexpectedly. The volume was down, so it was just an intense vibration in my hand that I quieted by answering once I saw the name on the screen.

Jude.

"Hey," I said, moving toward the front door. I peeked out, and realizing that there was enough light spilling from the window that it wouldn't be pitch dark, I stepped onto the covered porch and closed the door behind me to talk to my younger sister.

"You know your mother is getting on my nerves, right?" she asked, once we'd finished the usual opening pleasantries. "She's written a pretty tragic narrative about your little trip to the mountains in her head, and she is going over it in full detail to anybody who'll listen. Your nephew thinks he needs to get in contact with T'Challa and his folks to come and get you."

"Lord, she brought my baby in on the foolishness too?"

I relished the sound of my sister's laugh on the other end of the line. "Girl, nobody is safe, man woman or child. She told me she talked to you this morning."

"Yeah," I agreed, staring into the darkness past the porch. "Before I went to find my phone."

"Which I called you on, so I'll assume you either found it or said screw it and got a replacement."

I shook my head. "Nah... I found it."

"Good. That's one happy ending, at least. Other than that, how are you doing? I heard you *fell*? Are you okay?!"

"Yes, I'm fine, despite what your mother probably insinuated, there's no cast, no broken bones, none of that. Just a little bump on the head, and a few scrapes. Nothing to be concerned about."

"But you know I am anyway, right?"

I sighed. "Yes, Jude. I do. But I'm fine."

"You said you were fine for two years, and then—"

"Could we *not* go there?"

Jude sucked her teeth. "I mean, we don't *have* to, but when it's the whole reason your ass is up in the mountains anyway, well..."

"It's not the *whole* reason."

"Isn't it though?"

My response was interrupted by a clap of thunder as the storm intensified again, making me draw closer to the house.

"Where are you?" Jude asked. "Is it storming? Why is it so loud?"

"Because I'm outside," I sighed. "Stepped out for privacy."

I didn't have to be there to know that a deep furrow had appeared between Jude's eyebrows – I'd experienced it in person enough to recognize the change in tone that typically accompanied it. "... privacy? I thought your cabin *was* private?"

"My cabin is. But I'm not at *my* cabin. I'm at someone else's. It's a long story."

"Girl, DJ is somewhere downstairs wearing his daddy's nerves out while mommy has some me-time. Give me *all* the details. Where you at, heifer?!"

Even though it was damp with rain, I sank onto the wooden bench beside the front door as I launched into my tale of everything that had led to me ending up in Ben's house. My annoyance had – marginally – faded during the time I'd been talking to Jude, but now that he was the topic of conversation, it all came rushing back.

"I swear, Jude, I have *never* met a more infuriating person in my life. He's seriously the meanest, most arrogant asshole I've ever had the displeasure of *having* to deal with."

"Come on, Dr. Desmond," Jude teased. "*Ever?*"

"*Ever*," I confirmed, knowing she'd brought up the whole 'doctor' thing in disbelief that my clinical experience had *never* brought me in contact with someone more distasteful. "And I mean that. Because in the hospital setting, if it's the patient, it's like... okay, they're in pain, etc, so at least there's a *reason*. Or if they're racist or something, I can count you out as a dumbass, and keep it pushing. But there's *no reason* for this man to act the way he does toward me, and I think that's why it pisses me off so much. But he keeps stopping short of being completely evil, and somehow that makes me *more* mad. He's all the way under my damn skin, and I cannot *stand* it."

For a few moments, Jude was quiet, and then, "Is he cute?"

Immediately, I scoffed. "Is he... *what?!*" My face twisted into a scowl. "Why would you even ask me that? Why does that even matter? He's a rancid asshole of a human being – I can't say I've noticed if he's 'cute' or not."

"Bullshit," Jude challenged. "Personality aside, *is he cute?*"

"I..." I groaned, pulling his face up in my mind as I tried to do what my sister was asking – putting his horrific personality aside to consider his looks. My stomach flipped in disgust as I

CHRISTINA C JONES

came to terms that according to the picture in my head at least...
"Okay. He's... handsome. In a *he very likely steals candy from babies* kinda way."

"I *knew* it!" I rolled my eyes as, on the other end of the line, my sister broke into a peal of giggles. "Send me a picture!"

"Girl I don't have a damn *picture*," I scolded, shaking my head. "Why would I have a picture?!"

"Uh, because he's fine, and rescued you from the forest?" she said, as if that was some overly obvious answer. "But whatever. Describe him."

"I'm not about to—"

"*Describe him!*"

I grunted. "Fine. Um... he's tall. Fit. Chiseled features. Chocolate."

"*Mmmm,*" Jude moaned like she'd bitten into a honey bun. "He sounds delicious."

"That may be, but he's getting on my goddamned nerves."

"Even more reason that you should sample his dick tonight – you won't be tempted to go back for second helpings, because you hate his guts. I mean... unless he rearranges *your* guts a little *too* good, then you might have a problem on your hands."

Eyes wide, I countered, "Good thing there's exactly *no* chance of that happening then, huh? Jude, why would you even suggest that to me?! I didn't come up here for this!"

"Are you sure?"

"Yes! This trip was supposed to be about... getting in touch with myself again, and... *thawing.* I wanted to be human again, and... have emotions. *Feel something.*"

"Well then you may as well pack it up and come on home, because from where *I'm* sitting... it seems like Ben has you *feeling* plenty. So what if it isn't warm and fuzzy? Kyle, for the past two-and-a-half years, you have been... like a robot, with anybody who wasn't family. And even then, DJ has been the only person who gets much out of you. But the way you're talking about this 'Ben... I haven't heard you excited about *anybody*, in forever."

"*Excited* isn't the word I would use, when it comes to him. More like *incensed*."

"Okay so that's something. Better than the *nothing* you've been wallowing in, since... you don't need me to remind you. I'm just saying. Anger is still a feeling, so... ride that wave. And ride his dick."

"I am *not* about to entertain foolishness with you," I told her, shaking my head.

"It's not foolishness. A good orgasm would do you a world of good."

"Bye Jude."

"Bye sis!" she chuckled. "Don't forget to put a little curve in your back!"

I ended the call with my sister laughing in my ear, over something I didn't find all that funny. Not funny at all. There was *nothing* about Ben that made my brain go there, period, and certainly not enough to spur me into action.

He *did* look rather handsome with Dom sitting at his feet when I stepped back into the house to find him standing at the doorway that led from the foyer to the rest of the house.

"I thought you'd decided to tough it out in the storm until I saw your bag was still here," he said, some sort of tension I didn't recognize marring his tone.

"Were you listening to my conversation?" I asked, earning a scowl.

"No. I couldn't hear you well enough to eavesdrop if I wanted to – which I don't. I was waiting to make sure you got back inside."

I nodded, and didn't bother checking the sarcasm in my tone before I responded, "Right. Because of your *duty*."

"You're goddamn right, because of my *duty*," he snapped back, obviously not a fan of receiving the same snark he easily dished out. "You should consider yourself lucky – it's probably the only reason you're alive right now."

"Oh *forgive me*, please," I whined. "I am so sorry for not falling to my knees in adequate appreciation of all these things you've made abundantly clear you'd rather not have even done. How will you ever forgive me?"

As he usually did when he'd provoked me, he smirked. "I'd rather forget you."

"The feeling is overpoweringly mutual."

Ben's eyebrow lifted, and his gaze dropped to the front of my tee shirt. "Is it?"

I didn't have a chance to unravel that before he'd walked off, Domino trailing behind him. My eyes lowered to my shirt, bugging wide when I realized why he'd said what he said.

My nipples were on the highest of high alert.

It wasn't particularly cold outside *or* in the house, so I didn't have either of those as my excuse. Some women had nipples that got hard for innocuous reasons or were just that way all the time.

I didn't have either of *those* excuses either.

Jude must have gotten into my head!

That was the only explanation that made sense to me, for why I would have such a reaction to going back and forth with this man. I sank to a seat near my bag, baffled by my body's betrayal – especially when taking that seat made my state of arousal seem even more prominent.

At first, my brain went to when I'd sat down on the wet bench outside, which could easily be the culprit. But deep down, I knew better – this was a different wetness.

And it really, *really* pissed me off.

Sexual arousal was something I hadn't felt in so long that it was almost foreign to me, and *this* was a messed up way to get reacquainted. Even if I *had* come to Sugar Valley with the intention of some sort of sexual awakening, it was a cruel joke for *this man* to be the subject.

I didn't want to screw *him*.

I wanted to bludgeon him.

Ugh.

There was no reason to dwell on it.

I pulled out the phone, rechecking the weather radar, to see if Mother Nature was *sure* she wanted to keep this thunderstorm rolling. Unfortunately, the radar was all mottled red and orange, hanging over the area in a slow-moving storm current for the next several hours.

Meaning I was here until at least morning.

May as well settle in.

Digging through my bag, I found the little portable hygiene kit that had come with it. I hadn't even intended to use this backpack on the trip – I'd brought it as a backup, in case the other one got dirty or wet. *Cut off me to keep a bear from dragging me away* hadn't even crossed my mind.

In any case, I was glad to have it. All the products in the tiny kit were basic, stuff that I wouldn't regularly use, but something was better than nothing. I pulled out the vacuum-sealed change of clothes I hadn't yet opened – leggings, long sleeved tee shirt, underwear – and carried that, my hygiene bag, and my cell phone with me, venturing uninvited through the doorway that led to the rest of the house.

With everything going on before, I hadn't paid attention to the house itself, but now I did. It was beautifully done, with polished hardwood floors and exposed beams, and natural stone accents everywhere, including the fireplaces. The rustic design fit with where we were, while still being modern, with big windows and sleek furniture. It was... nice. *Really* nice.

And if I was honest with myself... so was the picture in front of me.

From the foyer, the space spread into the big open kitchen, which I'd been in before. It was empty. To my right, warmth and light spilled from the living room, where Ben was sprawled out on the couch, a beer bottle in his hand, and Domino spread across his lap. Both of their eyes were closed.

I couldn't stare at them too long, nor did I want to wake them, so I went about my business of finding a bathroom. There was a little three-quarter-bath off the kitchen, complete with towels. *Good* towels.

Finally, another win today.

Cranking the temperature of the water as hot as I could stand it, I climbed under the soothing spray of the water, not caring about soaking any bandages. I closed my eyes, taking a few moments to let the shower soak me through, washing away all the little worries and frustrations.

Temporarily, at least.

After a few minutes, I moved to the actual washing, then rinsed off. I didn't know what exactly the water situation was at the house with him being up on the mountain, but I didn't want to use all the hot water. Just because he was an unpleasant host, didn't mean I had to be a bad guest.

I dried myself off, then took on the task of replacing the bandaging on my knee, using the supplies I'd stuffed into the toiletry bag from my own first aid kit. Then, I wrestled my hair into the neatest braid I could without a comb or anything. I brushed my teeth, washed my face, and packed everything up before I finally got dressed, so I could head straight back to taking up as little space as possible in the foyer, and staying the hell out of Ben's way.

As soon as I opened the bathroom door, there was what

sounded like an explosion outside, and then everything turned black.

Please God, don't let this be my fault...

I didn't *think* I'd done anything that might have caused something like this, but still. Knowing Ben, he'd find a way to tie it to *something* I'd done wrong. I turned on my cell phone's flashlight feature, intending to use it to find my way back in the dark. I'd only gone a few steps before I heard a sharp bark that stopped me in my tracks, and then the blinding glare of a *real* flashlight was turned on me.

"Good, you're already up," Ben grunted, pulling me by the arm into the kitchen. "Sit here," he demanded. "So I know where you are. I need to go check on this transformer and make sure there aren't any power lines or anything across the road. Domino will stay with you."

My eyes widened. "Wait, you're going out there in this?!" I asked, pointing out at the steady, heavy downpour happening on the other side of the window. "I thought you said it was dangerous!"

"It *is* dangerous, but it's also necessary."

Anxiety spiked in my chest. What the hell was I supposed to do if he didn't come back?

"How long should it take?" I asked, hovering behind him as he pulled on a pair of coveralls from what I'd assumed was a pantry, and then slid his feet into heavy rain boots.

"An hour. Maybe two."

"You know what you're doing?"

I didn't even have to see his face to know I was wearing on his nerves, but surprisingly, he let it slide, picking up a heavy-looking bag of tools.

"Yes. Can I go now?"

I glanced around, taking a second to realize that I was in the way of him exiting the pantry. I moved back, and Ben said nothing else before he put on a head covering, then disappeared out the kitchen door.

Like he said, Domino stayed, but she damn sure didn't seem happy about it.

I felt bad for her as she paced back and forth in front of the door, for nearly ten minutes. Finally, she took a seat, her head pointed keenly in the direction where Ben had gone, not moving.

Get a grip, Kyle. Are you just going to sit here watching the dog?

Using my cellphone flashlight, I searched around the kitchen until I found candles and a lighter, using those to light the room.

And then I waited.

Feeling a little silly about it, honestly, hanging around this man's kitchen like a widow waiting on a soldier to return from war. He'd made his opinion of me *abundantly* clear, and his disdain was reciprocated, which made being worried about him more than a little pitiful.

Or... just human?

Care and compassion for strangers weren't exactly negative traits after all. Throughout my career in medicine, I'd become well-versed – working as a trauma surgeon quite literally put people's lives in your hands.

Compassion was *necessary*.

Or at least... I'd thought.

If nothing else, the last few years had taught me that it was, indeed, possible to do, and even excel at, my job without any real empathy for the people on the operating table. It wasn't that my concern had been replaced with contempt, or anything like that. The problem was that in place of the benevolent nature that had driven me to become a trauma surgeon in the first place, I'd become... apathetic.

Which was arguably worse.

I went about the business of saving lives through pure mechanism, using the intricacy of surgery after surgery as a conduit to hide from my own pain. I read every medical journal and wrote a few articles myself, picked up admin work, continuing education courses, whatever I could. Devoted myself, completely, to the singular task of never having a quiet enough moment to feel anything, for anyone, except my close family. I scrubbed into surgeries and rewired, removed, reattached, whatever was required of me, with absolute precision.

Until I crashed.

And now, my emotional wiring was so mixed up that I doubted myself for being concerned about a man going out into a dangerous storm to do necessary work that might keep someone from a life-threatening situation. So wholly disorganized that getting pissed off turned me on.

Defective.

I was still contemplating my faulty emotional state when Ben came back through the door, soaking wet and scowling. A quick glance at the time told me he'd been gone for closer to the two-hour end of the range he'd given before he left, a detail that probably contributed to Domino's reaction to his safe return.

She was all over him, and Ben didn't seem to mind – The scowl he'd been sporting on the way in was easily replaced with a wide grin as she jumped up, pawing and barking at him until he stopped his process of taking off his wet gear to give her some attention.

Once she was satisfied he was in one piece, she moved near where I was and took a seat – a subtle acceptance of my presence that she hadn't offered in the time he was gone. Ben seemed as surprised by it as I did, his eyebrows reaching way up before he shuttered his expression back to the usual indifference he held for me.

"So how did it go out there?" I asked, trying to make conversation. "I'm assuming there was work to be done, since it took you a while to get back?"

He shrugged. "Some sizable branches across the road, so I got those out of the way, in case anybody is trying to get through. The transformer is torched, but the power lines are intact."

"That's a relief, right? I can't imagine trying to deal with power lines in the rain would be an easy task."

"Nah," he shook his head. "Not really."

He finished stripping off his rain gear and then pulled off his shirt too, like I wasn't even there. I averted my gaze, not wanting to feed into Jude's teasing from earlier with the sight of broad shoulders and sculpted abs in the candlelight. He strode past me, into the darkness of the house, then returned a moment later with towels that he tossed on the floor where he'd left his gear, soaking up the puddle of rainwater and then wiping everything dry and clean before he returned it all to the pantry.

It was once his back was to me that I realized he was scarred.

Badly.

The telltale remnants of a serious fire had been left behind on his body, shiny and mottled, in direct contrast of the near flawlessness of the rest of his skin – I could tell where healthy skin had been removed, to facilitate grafts. The burn wrapped from his belly button around to his spine, extending as high as his armpit and going further than I could see under the waistband of his pants.

Curiosity tugged at me with many hands, but I found the restraint not to give in. Not while my empathy button was still broken. I wasn't new to burn victims – I'd done skin grafts, debridement, and other emergency procedures on patients with the absolute worst of burns, sometimes so severe that limbs had to be removed.

Sometimes too severe to recover from.

Because of that, I had to check myself – a healthy amount of decorum had been instilled in me since birth, and had been the thing that saved me from being branded cold by my patients. I knew how to act. I knew what not to say.

I knew better than to ask him about a possibly traumatic event not for his benefit, but for the sake of sating my own morbid professional interest.

But I must have been staring too hard.

"Is there something I can help you with?" he asked, frowning as he stood at the sink, washing his hands. "Or are you sitting there like a bump on a log for fun?"

I rolled my eyes. "Before you left, you demanded that I stay in here."

His eyes wide as he nodded, obviously remembering now. "Cool. So you *can* get something right. Nice."

"You're committed to this asshole role, huh?" I asked, leaving my barstool as he ambled in my direction. "You never break character?"

He smirked. "You shouldn't make it so damn easy, if it bothers you so much."

"Whatever," I snapped turning to walk away. But I'd only made it a few steps before I realized the now-familiar moisture between my legs, the heaviness in my breasts, the arousal prickling over my skin. Instead of stomping away, I turned, tipping my head back to look him right in the face, but... I didn't know what to say.

"What?" he asked, scornful as usual. "You're mad? You've got something to say? You're hungry again? What is it that you want from me, huh?"

"I want you to..." I took a deep breath, hesitating over my word choice before I met his gaze again, unwavering. "I want you to fuck me."

Bafflement broke through his normally confident gaze. "Excuse me?"

"You heard what I said. So..." I swallowed, hard. "Yes or no?"

He stared at me for a few moments, scrutinizing me with a slow sweep down my face, to my chest, which was covered with my tee shirt. A tremble ran up my spine as he slipped a hand underneath it, but instead of coming up, to my breasts, he went... down.

Into the waistband of my leggings, my panties, between my thighs. My knees weakened as he touched me there – the first time I'd been touched there in years —sinking into me before he withdrew, bringing his fingers to his nose to inhale.

I wanted to be offended.

I *was* offended but more than that, the arousal that darkened his eyes as he breathed me in only made me wetter.

"*Yes.*"

I took a reflexive step backward, inexplicably caught off guard by his answer. Sure, I'd asked, essentially putting myself up on a platter. But... it was just an idea – a reckless flight of fancy that became suddenly real with a simple one-word response.

I took another step back, and he took one toward me, brows furrowed. "So are we doing this or not?"

"Of course," I answered immediately, once more allowing my mouth to write a check my impulse control wasn't quite eager to cash. There was no turning back though – Ben easily lifted me up and over his shoulder, grabbing one of the lit candles to bring along as he ventured into another part of the house.

To his bedroom.

He closed the door behind him, putting the candle down on the nightstand before he tossed me onto the bed with a simple, two-word command: "Get naked."

But I didn't.

Instead, I watched *him* get naked, my uncertainty growing even more once my eyes landed on the dick I'd so valiantly offered a place inside of me for the night. Of course, he caught me looking, and that annoying ass smirk of his grew even more smug.

"You scared now?" he asked, approaching the bed. The deep brown of his skin seemed to glow in the flickering candlelight. Despite the scars, his body was beautiful, which made defiance of his words easy.

"Never."

"Then why are your clothes still on?"

"If you want them off, you can take them off yourself," I countered, trying my best to keep the tremble of nerves out of my voice.

I hadn't had sex in a long time. And it had been even longer, more than a decade, since I'd experienced the awkward wonderment of intimacy with a new partner. The fact that I didn't even *kinda sorta* like Ben was a further complication, of this already *kinda sorta* terrifying predicament that I'd talked my way into.

But I was no punk.

Hence, the shit talking, even though I was scared out of mind.

Luckily, he had enough bravado for both of us, boldly grabbing me by the ankles to pull me to the edge of the bed. Once I was there, he hooked the waistband of my leggings and panties at the same time, snatching them off me in one pull before he tossed them to the floor. My tee shirt was next, then my bra, and then I was completely naked, being stared at with hungry eyes by a man who was virtually a stranger.

Kyle... what the hell are you doing?

I couldn't answer that.

Not really.

Ben certainly knew what *he* was doing though, grabbing a condom from somewhere beside the bed, sliding it on before he spread my legs apart, and settled on top of me.

"You said you were staying a while, right?" he asked, so close that with every inhale, my hard nipples brushed the tiny hairs scattered across the broad plane of his chest.

I raised an eyebrow. "Yes. Why?"

"Because I want to make it clear... this is just sex. When you leave this bed, I'm not your boyfriend, your secret bae, none of that."

My face twisted into a scowl. "Uh, yeah, we're on the same page. Nobody is trying to lock you down – I didn't come here for that. So you don't have to worry abou—"

"Yeah, aiight, I got it," he interrupted, pushing up on hand and using the other to spread my legs wider for him to settle between. "This is only gonna work if you're *not* talking, so—"

"*Uggh!*" I grunted, shoving him off me. "You are *such* a goddamn jerk!" I yelled, getting even madder as he sprawled out on his back with an exasperated groan. I scoffed, then sat up on my knees beside him, glaring at him. "*You're* annoyed?"

"Uh, yeah! You're the one who asked to do this, and now you're bullshitting. I could've gone to bed and kept pretending you didn't exist, but nah, you had to – *oh, shiiiiit.*"

"Right," I jeered, taking a deep, fortifying breath as I sank further onto his dick. He opened his mouth to say something, and I put my hand over it, using the other as a counter-weight against his chest to keep me from going too far, too fast. "*Shut. Up,*" I told him, looking him right in the eyes. He was clearly amused – but apparently willing to play along, because he tucked his hands behind his head and gave the slightest of nods, indicating that it was my show.

The problem was, I was working with all brand-new material.

It's just like riding a bike, Kyle. Once you know, you never forget.

That was the pep talk I gave myself as I removed my hand from his mouth, anchoring it on his chest with my other hand. Then, I started moving my hips. Careful. Slow. At first, it hurt, but as I stretched to accommodate him, the pleasure came, and then muscle memory seemed to take over, and I couldn't help the giddiness in my chest.

It was probably a silly thing to be excited about, but *God* it felt amazing, and I didn't bother holding myself back from verbalizing it. I was... waking up. That's what it felt like. Even though I had my eyes shut tight, it was like finally breaking through a thick fog, and reconnecting with a small part of the woman I used to be.

Kyle Desmond had great sex.

Kyle Desmond got angry sometimes.

Who knew it would take one to unlock the other?

Pinning my knees to Ben's hips for leverage, I pressed up, removing my hands from his chest to grip my breasts instead, giving in to the need to cup, caress, and squeeze. They were only there for a moment before they were brushed aside, replaced with bigger hands.

Rougher hands.

Hotter hands.

My head tipped backward, eyes on the ceiling as he pulled and plucked my nipples, pinching them tight between his fingers. My mouth was open, moaning, pleading, screaming as I rode him harder, harder, *harder*, chasing the delicious ache of taking all of him, feeling him wholly submerged in me.

Feeling.

It was so, *so* good, so breathtakingly, excruciatingly good that I could have stayed like that forever, listening to him mutter about how wet I was, how good I felt, riding him with one hand between my legs, the other clutched around his shoulder as he tweaked my nipples so gloriously hard I couldn't take it, but definitely didn't want him to stop.

But then, there was the release.

The clutching of thighs, and tensing of shoulders, the guttural cry and the clenching of my belly as the orgasm surged through me, and the upward surge of Ben's hips as he came too.

I collapsed onto the bed, dazed and wrung out. Ben extricated himself from between my legs, but only long enough to dispose of the soggy condom and don a new one, then climbed back to me.

There was no warning before he plunged into me, with a deep, swift stroke that made me arch away from the bed. He didn't move, either. He stayed buried in me, filling me up, waiting until I'd settled before he grinned at me in the dim, flickering light from the candle.

"So it's true then, huh?" he asked, pulling out just far enough for me to enjoy a half-second of relief before he drilled into me again.

"What?" I gasped, grabbing and digging my nails into his shoulders.

"They say crazy women have the best pussy. Now I have real-life experience."

"I hate you so *much,*" I whimpered, squirming underneath him as he stroked me again, and again, and *again,* taking the bite out of my words. It was hard to declare your derision for someone when they were stroking you with the kind of precision that hit all the right places, places you'd forgotten you had, places that made you a little intoxicated.

He hooked an arm under my knee and raised it high, shifting angles to get deeper.

Okay.

Not a little intoxicated.

Completely, utterly lifted, with no desire to come down.

Ben draped one of my legs over his shoulder, and then the other, plunging so deep it felt like he was in my stomach. He pressed against my thighs, further, further, further, until they were pinned against my chest and he was damn near perpendicular on top of me, pushing and grinding, creating sweet, *sweet* friction against my clit.

But then he shifted again.

My free leg locked around his waist, his mouth on my neck, sucking and biting and kissing and stroking me in slow, carefully metered strokes that were so, *so* agonizingly good. Dipping to catch a sensitive, painfully rigid nipple between his teeth before he sucked it hard, sending a fresh jolt of pleasure through me.

My hands drifted lower. From his shoulders, to his back, and then, barely even conscious of it, my fingers were tracing the edges of that burn, discovering that it descended past his waist, marring his hip, spilling onto his ass, and not stopping until it reached the top of his thigh.

Ben stopped when I stopped.

I opened my eyes, taking in the sweat building along his brow before I dropped my gaze to meet his. The candle was dim, on the verge of flickering out – I couldn't read him.

"Go ahead. Ask."

It was a dare.

If I asked, he'd probably answer, but satisfying my curiosity would come with a price. I had a choice – did I want to venture down that rabbit hole, or did I want to stay here in *this* moment, of sweat, and sticky wetness, of pleasure, and skin on skin. And... obscurity.

"No."

There was no right or wrong answer, but... my answer was still correct. Ben brought his lips to mine – surprisingly, but not unwelcome. I was rediscovering, so there probably wasn't much I would have said no to, honestly, in favor of learning myself all over again.

Because I didn't pull away, I found out that I was very much a fan of his tongue in my mouth, licking and swiping, his teeth on my lips for gentle nips, my lip in his mouth, getting sucked like a popsicle.

And I really, *really* liked deep, slow kisses that matched deep, slow strokes, and I liked those things even more when they preceded fast, furious, breath-snatching plunges that made my eyes roll back and made me cum so hard I screamed myself hoarse, which *he* liked so much that he slammed into me hard enough to keep us permanently stuck that way when *he* came.

We rolled away from each other afterward, which I didn't mind.

At all.

I didn't need the stimulation of his touch while I was basking in the joy of my first orgasms in what felt like forever, while my mind was racing and wondering, while I was... *breathing*.

I felt amazing.

Maybe this trip was a good idea after all.

CHAPTER FOUR

I didn't have to kick her out.

She left of her own accord, and no lie... I was impressed.

I was so used to waking at five in the morning that my alarm was more of a backup than a necessity – which was good, since the power was still out. All I knew about Kyle's exit was that it happened between the time I'd finally exhausted myself of being inside her, and when I opened my eyes.

She even cleaned up after herself.

The only traces that she'd been there at all were the neatly folded towels she'd left on the sink after using them, and the soiled bandages in the trash can. The sight of *those* pricked at me enough to wonder if she'd made it safely out of the woods or not. Neither was a particularly severe injury, but after the way it stormed yesterday, the mountain wasn't a particularly safe place. If she left out the back door, she'd easily have noticed the garage, then the driveway, which led to the road, which led straight to Sugar Valley, and was only about a mile-long walk.

If she left out of the front though... there was a fair chance of ending up back in the woods, with the slick hiking trails, and snakes, and...

Shit.

I got Dom set up with her first meal of the day, then hunted down my cell phone to call my mother. That woman seemed to know damn near *everything* that happened in Sugar Valley – which was why I lived just outside of it. Surely though, if anyone knew where the new booty in town was, it was her.

"Yes, I'm fine. No, I don't need any help at the house. Yes, you're needed up at the lodge. No, I did not save you a plate. Should've brought your ass down the mountain if you were hungry," she trilled, getting her first goads of the day over with early as hell.

I frowned. "Dang, woman. That's how you greet your favorite son?"

"I wouldn't brag about that title too much, seeing as you're my *only* child."

"That's beside the point," I told her, sinking back into the comfort of my bed, but only staying reclined for a moment before I sat up – my sheets smelled like... Kyle. "You really didn't save me a plate?"

She chuckled. "Couldn't have if I wanted to. Your cousins swamped me last night, ate up a whole Boston butt."

"Greedy bastards."

"You're one to talk. Come on down here so I can get some breakfast in you before we start cleaning up."

The "cleaning up" she was referring to had nothing to do with walking around with a bucket of hot, soapy water and a sponge. It was the work we did after every significant storm, clearing away branches, roof repairs, relieving any flooding. Usually, it was mild, but if she felt the need to feed me beforehand, the town itself must've taken a substantial hit.

But... my mother was pretty much *always* trying to feed me, so perhaps that didn't mean what I thought it did.

"I'll be there in a few," I told her, getting up from the bed to pull the linens off. "Hey – you checked in on the lodge occupants yet? Everybody good? I need to bring any special tools?"

"Just your hands. There's a bit of flooding in the recreation space, but the residents are fine. That *hipster* couple is likely to work my goddamn nerves though, fussing about their air purifier not working cause the power's out. Take ya' ass outside, we're in the damn mountains!" she declared, and I pressed my lips together to keep from laughing. "I am a little worried about the doctor though. I don't think she's sleeping well with that head injury, and the storm couldn't have helped. She didn't answer when I knocked on her door yesterday, and then this morning, she answered looking like she'd been rode hard and put away wet."

I stopped moving, with the fitted sheet halfway off the bed. "Doctor?"

"Don't play with me boy, you're the one who carried her to Doc's office in your arms. That girl is pretty as a Georgia peach, you know who I'm talking about. Kyle Desmond."

"Yes, Mama. I just didn't know she was... a doctor."

I couldn't say what I *did* think she was, but it wasn't *that*. She seemed too... *something*... for that.

"Oh yes, a big city trauma surgeon. I looked up her name, found all kinds of articles with her name – stuff about her, stuff she wrote. She's supposed to be some kinda genius!"

Okay.

That shit nearly made me choke on my tongue trying not to laugh. Kyle Desmond was fine as hell, and the pussy was A-1, but a *genius*?

Nah.

Somebody was lying.

"Uh... good for her?" I coughed, trying to clear the laughter from my throat. "I'm going to let you go for now though Mama, so I can get ready. I'll see you in... thirty?"

"Alright. And bring my grandbaby. I've gotta love on her, since your mean ass won't ever convince a woman to give you any human grandchildren for me."

"Funny. Bye."

As soon as we were off the phone, I continued my task of getting the sheets off the bed, to rid them of the feminine scent the "genius" had left behind. I tossed those linens in the general direction of the laundry, then threw on some clothes.

I'd grudgingly replace the sheets with clean ones when I got back... or sleep on the bare mattress until I felt like doing right. Once my morning hygiene was out of the way, I whistled for Domino to follow me out to my truck. While she climbed in and got comfortable on the floor, I cleared the fallen branches from the open bed.

And cleared Kyle Desmond from my head.

There was work to do.

So IT TURNED out my mother *wasn't* feeding me just to be feeding me – Sugar Valley had seen better days. Even though my official capacity was a forest ranger, the town took precedence, so it was all hands on deck.

All hands including the Sugar Valley Fire Department, my former peers.

I saw those guys often enough, to have wings and beers at *Maple* when there was a prize fight or big game, the softball league, etc. Two, Marc and Todd, were family – the cousins that had eaten up everything at Mama's house – so they were fixtures in my life as well.

It was different working with them again though.

It *almost* made me miss being part of the department even though there was no searing blaze involved. Using gas-powered, fume-spewing power tools to saw fallen trees into pieces for removal, replacing oversized fuses to get the power back up, digging trenches to relieve flooded yards... it was back-breaking work, and I loved every second of it.

Work made it hard to over think shit.

To think about anything except what you were doing, period.

It was glorious.

Still, when Todd smacked me on the shoulder, getting my attention before I swung the power saw one more time, I was glad to know it was time for lunch. The pancakes and sausage for breakfast were long gone, and the impromptu lunch service the town had arranged was calling my name, especially once I heard Doris Jones, who ran the diner, had provided the food.

I'd never admitted it out loud, but her food was even better than my mama's, which was a *high* compliment, because Mama threw down. It wasn't exactly an unpopular opinion either, considering their long-running tie in every food competition Sugar Valley had ever seen.

In any case... my mouth and stomach were ready for it.

With my cousins in tow, we headed to the cleanup station, scrubbing our hands before we joined the cafeteria-style line. My eyes were on the food, craning my neck to see what was on the menu... like my cousins, except they weren't scoping out the actual food.

"Who the hell is *that*?" Todd groaned, with Marc ad-libbing "*goddamn*".

I looked up, following their gaze to my mother at first, and I was ready to ask what the hell was wrong with those dudes until I stepped to where they were, and realized who they were looking at.

Shit.

"The future mother of my children," Marc said, eyes narrowed in an appreciative scowl as he stared Kyle down. I couldn't front – she looked... good. Better than she had the times I'd seen her before – even though now, I could be looking through pussy-colored glasses. She was undeniably more put-together though, with her hair down, hiding her bandaged head, clothes that weren't meant for hiking, fitted to her body, and... a smile.

That was probably the most significant difference, honestly.

There was happiness in her face as she used gloved hands to hand out rolls, talking for a moment with each person she served. My eyes shifted to my mother, who was standing next to her chatting away too, and I panicked, not knowing what Kyle might say once we made it to that part of the line. It took *nothing* for Mama to get an idea in her head when it came to me and women, and once she was latched on, she didn't let go.

If Kyle was hostile, my mother would be on it.

If Kyle was perfectly polite, my mother would be on it.

If Kyle said nothing, just handed me my roll and moved on the next person in line... Mama would *never* take her claws out of me.

How badly do I want this plate?

"Hey babies!"

I'd been so absorbed working out those scenarios I hadn't even noticed my mother leave the food service line and pop up where I was standing with my cousins. When I hazarded a glance at Kyle, she was now serving the rolls *and* the potato salad, which my mother had apparently abandoned to come speak to us.

"Not too much left to do," she happily sang, looking around. "We got this place whipped together in no time."

"Sugar Valley Fire Department is *always* glad to be of service."

Those words didn't come from me or either of my cousins – they came from Henry Chisolm, Fire Chief. I'd worked with the man for years, respected him, but the way my mother blushed over his presence, getting all giggly and high-pitched when he put his arm around her... it kinda made me want to punch him in the neck.

"You have been such a godsend to this town," Mama gushed, seeming to be in no hurry to leave his grasp. "As a matter of fact, I'm glad I caught you – you don't have to eat this picnic food. I've got yams and greens and cornbread and a thick slice of Boston butt from last night, just for you. I saved you a plate."

"*What*?!" I asked, out loud, earning a scolding glance from Mama, but seriously... *what*?! It hadn't even been six hours since that woman told me she hadn't saved any plates, but *this* motherfu—

"Alright I'll see you boys later!"

Before I could respond, she was hurrying off, with her arm looped through Chief Chisolm's, leaving me open-mouthed and betrayed. Marc and Todd thought the shit was funny, but it only took one stern look to cool *that* off.

I didn't play about my Mama.

Not that I was ever exactly a bundle of sunshine anyway, that whole interaction tanked my mood to the point that by the time we made it in front of Kyle, I didn't have shit for her... other than the scowl I probably would've offered anyway.

My cousins, on the other hand...

"So... never seen you around here before. What's your name, Beautiful?" Marc asked, leaning further over the service table than necessary.

"Kyle," she told him, offering a smile I didn't know her well enough to determine if she was just being polite or not.

"*Kyle*," Todd repeated, licking his lips.

This dude...

"Is that short for something? Kylindria, Kylista, Kyl—"

"No," Kyle laughed, wrinkling her nose. "Just regular ol' Kyle. I was named after an uncle who passed before I was born, and so was my sister."

"Sister, huh?" Marc and Todd both leaned in a bit more. "What's her name?"

"Jude."

Marc nodded. "Okay, I see. I like that. The name doesn't make the woman, the woman makes the name, all that. And from what I can tell, you're making the hell out of that name."

Her eyebrows lifted, and confusion marred her smile. "Is *that* right?"

"Hell yeah," Todd answered. "Tell me something... does Jude look like you?"

"Jude is actually the pretty one."

"That's wassup'," Marc drawled. "So uh... you and Jude... what are y'all getting up to tonight? Power's back on, and I don't see a ring on your finger, so..."

Kyle grabbed her left hand with the right, running her thumb over the inside of her ring finger. "Well... Jude is in Blackwood, and probably plans to spend the night with her husband and son, and I... just wanna serve the potato salad."

"Y'all are holding up the line with this wack ass game," I spoke up for the first time. "She blocked your shot, get your food and move, I'm hungry."

"Hater," Todd accused, holding up his plate. "Can I have two scoops please?"

Kyle's smile came back, and she nodded. "Big strong guy like you? Of course." Marc and Todd moved on through the line, making it my turn. Kyle looked me right in the eyes with confidence. "One scoop or two?"

"One."

Without taking her gaze off mine, Kyle dumped a perfect scoop of potato salad on my plate, then placed a roll beside it.

"*Enjoy*," she said, in a tone that probably sounded polite to the person behind me, but with the challenging ass eye-contact she was giving me, and the twitch in her eyebrow, I heard something different. Something more like, "*choke*".

"Thank you."

In unison, our gaze broke – we dismissed each other. I trailed my cousins to a table, putting food in my mouth before I even sat down. Marc and Todd were all over this "Kyle" situation, while I would rather talk about pretty much anything else. It didn't seem like they were interested in letting me stay out of it though.

"Why are you being all quiet and shit Benny?" Marc teased. "You mad we were trying to kick some brotherly game, you salty cause you got excluded?"

I damn near choked on a mouthful of chicken and had to clear my throat before I spoke. "*Please* exclude me from the narrative anytime you open your mouth to let garbage spill out. Cause that's exactly what your game is – garbage. Both of you."

Todd laughed. "Whatever dude, you watch and see – I'm gonna find out how long she's in town, and then I'm tearing that ass *up* before she leaves."

"Not if I get to her first," Marc challenged, guzzling down half a glass of cold lemonade. "I mean... I *saw* her first, so that's pretty much dibs."

"You're a saw her first *lie*. I'm the one who pointed her out!"

"Revisionist history dude, you know damn well—"

"*Actually*," I spoke, tired of the back and forth. "*I* saw her first. Two days ago. *I* hit it first. Last night. All night."

Todd sucked his teeth. "Nah, man. You lying, right?"

I shrugged, sitting back as I ripped off a chunk of my roll, preparing to put it in my mouth. "I've never lied on my dick before, don't plan to start now."

"Man, that's so *hateful*," Marc groaned. "We supposed to be family, and you do me like this?!"

Scowling, I leaned forward. "Knocking down a broad you'd never even seen or heard of before was hateful?"

"Hell yeah. *Look at her*! You should've known that was all me, should've known I'd want her."

I grunted. "Yeah. You and everybody else."

From where I was sitting, I still saw Kyle – could see her grinning at the apparent flirting of yet another man shooting his shot.

Unsuccessfully.

She shook her head at something he said to her and he clutched his chest, pretending to be physically wounded by her rejection. Kyle laughed at that, then held up her serving spoon with one hand, a roll in the other, dismissing him in the same manner she'd used with Marc and Todd – reminding him what she was standing there for.

"So you got details or nah?" Todd asked, leaning in.

"Or *nah*," I told him, shaking my head. "File that under *not your goddamn business*."

Obviously ignoring the fact that me sleeping with her at all wasn't their business either.

"Ben's stingy ass ain't telling *shit*," Marc laughed. "He only names names to stake his claim and let us know a chick is off limits."

"No claim has been staked," I corrected, shaking my head. "A fact was stated. That's all."

Todd scoffed. "So, you're not gonna trip if I try to get those draws?"

"Not at all," I assured. "I'm gonna *laugh*, absolutely, because she already smacked your shot into the stratosphere, but *trip*? Nah."

Some other guys from the firehouse and police station joined the table, so the conversation – mercifully – shifted to something else.

Anything else.

When I was finished eating, I cleared my place and then took everything to the trash and recycling bins before I headed back to my work from before. *Almost* done wasn't *done*, and once I finished what I was doing in town, I still had the trails to deal with.

Halfway to my destination, I ran into a face I wished wasn't so damn familiar. The woman brightened as soon as she saw me, and I forced a smile of my own, not wanting to be rude. It was something I only gave a damn about with a few people, and the Shaws were on that list.

"You doin' alright honey?" Donna Shaw asked me, putting down the bundle of fallen branches she was carrying to pull me into a hug. "I was just telling Scott how we don't ever see you anymore!"

By design, I thought, but didn't verbalize, as I submitted to her embrace. I squeezed her back, then stepped to look around. "Where is he? Somewhere keeping Nadia entertained?"

Donna grinned. "You already know. She started third grade this year, and all she does is talk talk talk. I couldn't take it with the school closed today. I told Scott, *you* stay here, *I'll* go help clean up in town. She can talk *his* ear off while they clean up the yard."

"Were you hit bad?"

"Oh, not at all," Donna said, waving me off. "Not nearly as many trees as we had at the other house. Up there, we had to clean fallen branches every time the wind blew. Ask Devin, I used to pay him extra allowance to... to..." Donna trailed off, blinking as she realized what she'd said. Very suddenly, her eyes were wet, and she bent to pick up the branches she'd been holding earlier. "Well... anyway. It was good to see you, okay? You take care of yourself, and... don't be a stranger. You'll *always* have a seat at our dinner table. Okay?"

"Yes ma'am," I agreed, knowing I would never set foot in their house, let alone sit down for dinner. Her invitation was genuine, and I appreciated it, but... I was good.

And I was anxious to get away from her.

My goodbye was quick – probably bordering on cold, but I couldn't look at her without thinking about shit I didn't want to think about.

It was time to get back to work.

And work so hard it was all I could think about.

CHAPTER FIVE

S ugar Valley was... an anomaly.

In the best possible way.

Of course I'd seen communities rally together, typically after much worse than a severe thunderstorm, but you'd think the town had been ravaged from the way they went all hands on deck. It didn't even seem to take much oversight – these people were working cheerfully to put their home in order, everybody had a place. I, however, was an outsider, supposedly here on vacation. When I finally woke up from the deep sleep I'd fallen into after her early morning check-in, I sought Regina for instructions. I wanted to help.

When she asked, I blamed my stunted stride on the fall I'd taken. Was I *dying* to talk to someone about the delicious soreness between my legs? *Absolutely.* Was that person going to be a woman I'd known for two or three days? *Absolutely not.*

I was talking *Jude's* ear off about it though, as soon as I had a chance.

In the meantime, I was cleaning up after the lunch service for the volunteers. This was yet another thing I'd marveled over – how quickly this was all pulled together and run so smoothly.

Even the tension I'd sensed between Regina and Doris, the woman who had provided all the food, didn't slow anything down. They kept a healthy distance from each other and did what needed to be done.

"My goodness!" I heard Regina's voice behind me as if I'd thought her up, and when I turned from picking up a stray paper plate, she was rushing in my direction. "I lost track of time," she said, smoothing her – ordinarily neat - hair back from her face. Now, it was barely holding on to the bun it had been in last time I saw her, and she seemed a little... flushed.

"Are you okay?" I asked, concerned about the tiny beads of sweat on her forehead. The storm had pushed a cold front through, bringing the temperature to mid-fifties at best.

"Yes," she quickly assured, pushing out a breath. "Just a little winded. I rushed back down when I saw the time. I see Ben is already gone, I wanted to introduce you."

"Oh, we've met." I shook my head, thinking back on even today's interactions, as minimal as they were. More than once, I'd felt the man's eyes on me, but he'd barely found two words to say to my face. Which was fine, considering his apparent ongoing competition with himself to say *the* most asshole things.

My words must've held a tone, because Regina's eyes widened. "You have?"

"Unfortunately. And I have to say – I fully understand why you warned me not to bother thanking him for that whole mountain rescue thing."

Regina laughed. "Yes, that boy can be... a little abrasive."

"A little abrasive?"

I laughed at that. Calling Ben "a little abrasive" was like calling the Earth "a little rock". Both were gross understatements.

"*More like the rudest sonofabitch I've ever met,*" I muttered, more to myself than anything, as I bent to grab a napkin from underneath one of the tables. When I straightened, Regina's eyes were brimming with delight, and her lips were pressed together like she was trying her best not to laugh.

My first thought was Ben standing over my shoulder, having overheard the conversation. But when I looked around, it was just me and her.

"What is it?" I asked, which apparently struck her as so funny she couldn't hold it anymore, her shoulders bouncing as she openly laughed, then finally met my gaze with wet, amused eyes.

"Well, it's just... I wouldn't call *myself* a bitch, but if you've been talking to Doris, there's no telling what she may have said."

I squinted. "Huh?"

Regina didn't answer, just laughed more, forcing me to consider what she'd said. And then, what *I'd* said.

And then...

"Oh, damn."

That made her laugh even harder as embarrassed heat crept up my face.

"Regina, I am *so*—"

"Don't you dare apologize," she stopped chuckling long enough to say, grabbing my free hand and squeezing. "Honey, I am keenly aware of who my son is, and the kinds of things that come out of his mouth. I'd almost be more concerned if you *didn't* think he was a jerk."

"Still," I shook my head. "If I'd known you were his mother, I would have..."

"Lied?" Regina laughed again. "One thing you don't ever have to do around me is mince words, especially about my child – you said it yourself, I warned you! You want to tell me what he did?"

"That's *not* necessary," I assured. I was a big girl, I could handle Ben without needing to tell his mother on him. "I need to spend some time researching how *not* to end up needing to be rescued from 'Big Sugar' up there."

"And I've already told you, falls, poison ivy, insect bites, getting tangled up in the trees, so on and so forth – I told you, that's everyday stuff around here."

I snorted. "*Ben* sure makes it seem like it isn't. Like you have to be an idiot for something to happen to you up there."

"Lord." Regina rolled her eyes. "You can't take that personal honey. He thinks everybody who comes to this mountain without having grown up on it is an idiot."

"That may be so, but still... I'll be here for an extended time. I should be able to take care of myself."

Aside from the obvious *don't ignore it when the sign says the trails are closed,* I needed... help. Even with all the reading I'd done before booking my trip, I hadn't been prepared for the deceptive difficulty of Sugar Leaf Mountain. All the reviews called it an "intermediate" hike, but I was starting to wonder exactly how relative that was. My fitness level wasn't the issue here though – the question was my skill level.

I had no skills.

"You know what you should do," Regina suggested, her lips spreading into a smile. "You should take the wilderness class!"

"Wilderness class?"

She nodded. "Yes ma'am! We offer it through the lodge, no extra charge for guests! It covers finding water, building a shelter, navigating in the woods, how to safely build a fire, a little basic hunting and edible plants, reading the weather – it's a wonderful program, really."

"It sounds like exactly what I need, how do I sign up?"

"I'll have the front desk get in touch with you as soon as we get everything back up and running. Actually – I need to be checking on that, now that the power is back on."

"Of course, go ahead," I urged. "I have to finish up out here. Don't forget about me with the class though."

"I won't honey," Regina said, with a quick side hug as she headed off.

Bending to grab another napkin from the ground, a smile spread over my face as I imagined myself coming out of class as some skilled woman of the woods. Mud on my face, a wolf I'd tracked and killed slung over my shoulder, wearing a leather dress and boots like Xena.

I laughed at myself as I moved to the next thing to be cleaned, allowing those happy thoughts to build on the positive feelings from last night's sexcapades. No, my trip hadn't started off exactly as I'd intended, but there had been good moments, which I chose to hold on to. This class was going to teach me what I needed to know to safely spend as much time as I could in the woods, for the rest of my stay.

I'd come to this mountain for something, and I wasn't leaving until I got it.

"THOSE WHO CAN, do. Those who can't... gotta get up in three hours to get ready to teach these fifth graders about mitochondria, woman."

I giggled at his response to me slipping underneath the covers and sidling right up to him, fresh from the shower and completely nude. It had been a long night at the hospital. I was tired, and he undoubtedly was too.

But, still.

I wanted him, and if his warm hands sliding up my body were any indication, it was mutual. He always complained about me waking him at three in the morning for this, but he never denied me. It was selfish, but he never held it against me. And because of that...

"I'll make it worth it," I promised in a whisper as he rolled to his back, pulling me on top of him. My hands slipped between us, freeing him from his boxers. "I love you."

Shit.

Shit, shit, shit.

I sat up in the bed, swallowing the reflexive panic of waking up in a room I still wasn't quite accustomed to, even though I'd been at the lodge for over a week now. Closing my eyes, I willed myself to get out of bed, to not give in to the overwhelming urge to look to the other side of the bed, listen for footsteps in the hall, or breathe in deep, hoping for a familiar aroma.

I couldn't help it.

My gaze fell on nothing except disheveled covers, my ears rang with a deafening silence, and the only thing I smelled was the wine I'd spilled on myself the night before but had been too trifling to change my sleep shirt.

Shit.

I got out of bed, refusing to take the time to sit with the disappointment I'd brought upon myself.

Wasn't that the whole point of coming up here, girl?

Whatever.

Brushing that thought away, I took the hottest shower I could stand and then brushed my teeth and washed my face. In the bathroom mirror, I stared at the cut on my head, going back and forth over whether to re-bandage it, torn between my knowledge that keeping it covered and moist would let it heal faster and be less likely to leave a scar, and my overwhelming desire to *not* look like a clumsy child at this wilderness class.

Ultimately, vanity won.

Instead of the bandage, I chose a wide headband that covered a good portion of the gash leading into my hairline, then left out enough hair in the front to hide the rest before I pulled the remaining hair into a low bun. Once I was satisfied with that, I dressed for hiking in the way the class description had suggested, then devoured a quick breakfast of Greek yogurt and granola before I headed out.

The cold front from last week's weather was still hanging around, so the air was crisp when I stepped off the front porch of my cabin for the short walk up to the main lodge. Looking around, any other remnants of the storm – fallen branches, roof shingles, and so on – were gone, leaving *Sugar Leaf Lodge* as postcard-image ready as it had been the day I arrived.

When I walked into the main building, I stopped at the front desk to ask where I needed to go for the class. I was pointed to a room styled as a small auditorium, with bench style seating and a little raised platform at the front, presumably for a moderator. The stage was set in front of the floor to ceiling windows that looked down over a dip in the mountain I hadn't realized was there. I went up to peek out, marveling at the view in the distance for a few moments before I took a seat. It was a little early, but I wasn't the first one there.

There were a few couples, and a family of four, but the rest of us appeared to be alone. Once I was seated, I closed my eyes, mentally preparing myself for whatever was about to happen – hoping it wouldn't end in another embarrassing episode. I was still mulling that over when I felt a shift in the air nearby. When I opened my eyes and looked up, someone was already sitting down.

"This seat wasn't taken, was it?" he asked, flashing me a smile.

No, the seat wasn't taken, but there were about fifteen others available, including the empty benches in front of and behind me. But of course, he'd chosen the seat he wanted.

"No," I answered, returning his smile because it was the

polite thing to do, completely unrelated to his handsome, clean-shaven face, and butter-pecan skin. "Consider it yours."

"Thanks. I'm Morgan." He offered his hand, and for a moment I looked at it, as if I'd never been offered this sort of greeting before. Like it was foreign.

I blinked, snapping out of the awkwardness I hoped hadn't lasted as long as it felt to accept his hand. "I'm Kyle." I wasn't surprised by the way his eyebrows lifted when he heard my name – it happened with everyone. "It's a family thing," I explained. "My mother and father both lost brothers at a young age, and they named my sister and me after them."

He nodded. "Ah, I see. You must get interesting reactions about it often."

"Yes. My absolute favorite is when patients see *Kyle Desmond* on the paperwork, and then *I* walk in – of course they assume I'm the nurse, because of course this Black woman can't be the surgeon, and then I correct it and suddenly the whole mood shifts." I shook my head. "Not that there's anything wrong with being a nurse – they're the ones who keep these people alive after I'm done with the knives and all. But still – why is it so hard to believe I'm the doctor? I've had people demand to see my ID before, and... I am talking your ear off right now, and offering way too much information, I'm sorry."

"Nah," he laughed. "Please, go on."

"I've said quite enough," I told him, shaking my head. "You know my full government name, family history, job title, and all I know is you're... Morgan."

He grinned, flashing perfect teeth to match the perfect face. "I can fix that. I'm Morgan Lewis. My father was... a rolling stone. So I have a metric ton of siblings. Most accurately, my job title is broke artist. I'm here to find inspiration. You?"

"Um... that is... a question I have no idea how to answer in a way that makes sense to anyone but myself."

"That's a polite way of telling me to mind my business," he laughed. "But I am going to accept that, and hope you'll feel like sharing another time."

Before I could respond, there was movement at the front of the room that caught my attention. It was a dog – a familiar, black and white dog, followed by her owner.

Domino and Ben.

"This isn't some cutesy class for you to share on your social media," he started – obviously indifferent to the fact that it was too early in the morning to be an asshole. "As a matter of fact, if it were up to me, I'd confiscate your phones, but the only person who can tell me what to do, said that was taking things too far. So you can keep them. What you *can't* do, is pose for selfies, 'do it for the gram', or anything of that nature, while you are under my instruction. If I catch you doing it, I will send you back to the lodge. Everybody clear on that?"

He only got a few sleepy grumbles in response, but that didn't seem to phase him as he smacked his hands, then rubbed them together. "Okay, let's get started – you were supposed to pack a bag, but there were no guidelines offered. I want you to empty that bag in front of you, and line it all up. I'm going to come by and check you out, one by one."

I rolled my eyes.

Of course Ben was the instructor for the wilderness class, and *of course* Regina hadn't felt the need to give me at least a *little* warning about it. Part of me wanted to get up and walk out, to not even subject myself to a whole weekend of Ben. But the other part refused to back down, especially not as an avoidance tactic.

Especially not when I was perfectly willing to give him back every ounce of snark he offered me.

"Who jizzed in this guy's grits this morning?" Morgan muttered, leaning in as he removed stuff from his bag.

I shook my head. "Get used to it. I'm pretty sure he thinks he's Major Payne, so..."

Morgan chuckled, and I sat back to empty my own bag, stealing little glances in his direction when I could. Not because he was so great to look at – even though he *was* great to look at – but more so because I was trying to figure out what the *hell* the little fluttery feeling in my chest was.

Hoe tingles, Kyle.

That's what they are.

What else *could* they be?

In the seven or eight days since I'd been in Sugar Valley, I'd already screwed one guy, and now here I was, hot in the face and over sharing like an idiot because of an entirely different one.

This was *not* what I was here for.

This wasn't even who I was – Kyle Desmond didn't giggle and flirt, especially not with complete strangers.

But that's assuming you're the same Kyle Desmond you've always been, and well... you can't be her. Not the woman you've been for the last few years, and not the woman you were before that. And wasn't this trip supposed to be about rediscovery anyway.

I pushed out a breath.

Right.

Teaching myself how to feel again, interacting like a reasonable person, and... yes... rediscovery. All those things had contributed, to some degree, to my taking this trip in the first place, but it didn't change the fact that it was all so much easier said than done.

Especially when deep, deep down, there was this question lingering, a sharp pin hovering just out of striking distance, waiting for the right moment to burst the balloon of any happiness you dared to feel.

Why should you get to be happy anyway?

What have you done to deserve to smile?

Shouldn't you be somewhere crying?

The weight of it all was enough to swallow me, make me wonder why I was doing this to myself. I never had to worry about those things – none of them even occurred to me – when I packed my emotions down, suffocating and suppressing until they were merely a pill to swallow.

Bitter or not, I'd choose it again.

"Kyle Desmond, you're up."

I blinked and looked up to find Ben in front of me with a clipboard. Shrugging, I sat back, letting him look over the inventory of my bag. Just as he had with everyone else, he poked around, occasionally checking things off before he moved on to the next person, without saying much of anything.

Officially making it probably the nicest interaction I'd had with him.

When he'd looked over everyone's bags, he stepped back to the front. His expression was a vague mix of disgust and disappointment when he spoke up.

"There are *ten* essentials you should have in your pack, every single time you step out of modern civilization, into the wilderness. Those same ten essentials make a great emergency bag to keep in your car and or home as well – that's free advice you should take advantage of – *after* I teach you these essentials. Unfortunately, there's only one person in this room besides me who has those fundamentals packed."

I rolled my eyes, looking around me to pinpoint who looked adequately prepared enough to earn a compliment from his royal ass-ness, landing on an older man whose pack looked as if it had been on plenty adventures.

"Kyle Desmond – you get the honor of standing up and

demonstrating the contents of your pack, as I go through this list."

My eyes widened, and I froze.

Me?

I didn't have too much time to think about it because Ben wasn't waiting around for me to get over my shock – he was moving on with the class. Like the good student I'd always been, I stood, holding up the corresponding item as he ran through a description of each "essential" – navigation, lighting, first aid, sun protection, rain protection/shelter, fire, knife, food, clothing, water – and all the various options we had for each thing.

"Sit down," Ben said, abruptly dismissing me from my unasked-for position as a showgirl. "The rest of you have thirty minutes to get whatever you don't have, and report back. We set out at the top of the hour, exactly, and I *will* leave you behind. Get up, get it done."

As everyone else gathered their things to follow Ben's instruction, I took my seat, watching.

"So you're *that* girl, huh?" Morgan asked, shooting me another grin as he closed his bag. "On the teacher's good side first thing?"

I scoffed. "I don't know about all that. What do you have to get?"

"Fire supplies and a flashlight. Got both back at my cabin, didn't think I'd need either."

"Makes sense. I called myself *over* preparing, after two... unsuccessful trips up the mountain, in the short time I've been here."

"You'll have to tell me those stories sometime."

I returned his smile, with a bit of a nod. "Yeah. Maybe so."

"Lewis!" Ben called, from the front of the classroom. He tossed his hands up. "You coming on this hike or not, brother?"

"I'm heading to get my missing supplies as we speak."

Morgan threw me a wink before he turned to leave, and after a moment, I realized his exit resulted in me being alone in the classroom with Ben – a situation I had little interest in being in.

A situation I didn't *have* to be in, since I only needed to be present by the same deadline everyone else had. With that in mind, I closed my bag, hefting it onto my shoulders before I stood to leave.

"I guess there might be *some* hope for you, Desmond," I heard, as I approached the door. When I stopped, to look over my shoulder, Ben wasn't even looking at me. He was looking out the window.

Against my better judgment – which I was very, very good at – I took a step back. "Is that a compliment?"

"It's an observation."

"An unexpected one, based on your tone."

One eyebrow was raised when he turned halfway, looking at me. "You seem surprised by that, but I can't imagine why. Have I *not* saved your ass on the mountain twice?"

"The first time was a freak accident. The second time, I was only up there because I needed something I'd lost the first time. I was afraid it would be lost to me forever if I didn't get it as soon as I could."

"That doesn't change the *facts*."

I shrugged. "Sure, I'll give you that, but it *definitely* creates some much-needed nuance, since you want to treat me like I'm stupid."

"I've never said you were stupid."

"But you certainly *thought* it," I accused, and he didn't argue against it because he *couldn't* argue against it. "I've made mistakes up there, absolutely, no argument there. And really... you can *think* whatever you want about me. I don't give a shit. But you will *not* speak as if I'm not one of the most brilliant minds *you* have ever had the privilege of being acquainted with."

By this time, Ben had turned to face me, eyebrows lifted. Once I stopped speaking, a smirk spread across his lips, and he gave me a single nod. "Fair enough," he conceded, ambling toward me, with his clipboard still clutched in one hand. "I won't talk to you as if you're stupid. But let's be clear – that doesn't mean you're going to start liking what I have to say. I still don't like you. I still don't believe you belong on this mountain. I'll still be glad when you leave."

I smiled down at Domino, who had apparently recognized me, and walked up to push her head under my hand. Giving her an affectionate rub, I returned my gaze to her owner, and let the smile drop from my lips.

"It's a good thing I don't give a damn what you believe, because I'm not here for your pleasure."

"Whose pleasure *are* you here for?" he asked, his gaze dropping to my lips and lingering there before he met my eyes. "Ol' boy that was grinning in your face?"

"My own."

"Mm." He was so close now I could feel the heat from his body, and every breath I took was a subtle inhalation of his aroma – a dual assault on my senses that brought back memories of the night I'd spent at his cabin.

Apparently, that night was on *his* mind as well.

"Your place or mine?"

My eyebrow lifted. "Excuse me?"

"You said you were here for your pleasure, and well... I think we both remember exactly how much you enjoyed yourself that night."

"One night is nothing," I shot back. "Anybody can be good for one night. A fluke."

He chuckled. "Nothing about this dick is a fluke. Maybe a *gift* if you need something to call it."

"Two minutes ago you were making sure I know you don't even like me."

"I don't need to *like* you, to make you cum."

"I'm ready now!" someone behind me gushed, from the classroom door. That interruption saved me from responding to Ben's words – or so I thought.

He grabbed the hanging part of one of the straps on my bag, using it to keep me from escaping as he replied to the student rejoining the class.

"Desmond," he said, clearly intent on getting an answer. "Yours or mine?"

"Neither," I told him, drawing the strength to resist from the fact that this conversation was much less private now, as the room started to fill again. I pulled away, knowing he couldn't hang on too tight unless he was willing to make a scene, which I doubted.

I was right.

I shot him a smirk as I moved away, practically walking right into Morgan as he re-entered the room.

"I am now fully prepared," he declared, momentarily grabbing me by the arms to make sure I stayed upright.

I smiled at him – because I was grateful for the assistance, and because Ben was watching.

"Perfect," I told him, then looked to Ben, who was wearing exactly the glare I expected. "Let's hike!"

CHAPTER SIX

I overplayed my hand.

I knew it from the moment Kyle walked away from my offer, and so did she, probably.

The way I saw it, I had two options from there – keep pushing, or fall back and mentally regroup. So really... one option.

Fall back.

Mostly because I didn't even understand what was going on. *Me,* sweating a woman? Nah. That was some shit that flat out didn't happen, and I didn't plan to start now, especially not with a woman who didn't even have basic ass common sen—

She told you about that shit, remember?

Right.

"...one of the most brilliant minds you've had the pleasure of being acquainted with."

The confidence to tell a near-stranger such a thing interested me more than anything else about her, to be honest. I employed a healthy level of shit-talking from day to day, so a woman who engaged with that, and utilized some of her own... a woman who didn't back from it, and simply gave back the same energy she was given...

Of course I wanted her again.

How could I not?

But you've already had her...

Yeah.

For one night, which was usually enough.

Sometimes, a few nights, if it seemed like they could manage without any pesky feelings getting involved. We got what we wanted and moved on, no hard feelings – at least not on my part.

There was... something else going on here though.

Something I didn't like. Something way too close to the possibility I was actually... maybe... *feeling her*.

Which pissed me off.

It pissed me off that *"Morgan"* was all in her face, jumping at the chance to be her partner when I had the group pair into twos for the fire-building segment. They did entirely too much giggling through the process of teaching them how to purify water, but they got the shit right, so I couldn't say much.

I *did* almost put his ass out of class for his corny ass rendition of *"Location"* in the middle of me trying to teach the group how to navigate in the woods. Kyle was *way* too amused by that shit.

Which pissed me off.

Neither one of them fashioned a shelter worth a damn, but they managed to at least signal for rescue and put a band-aid on. During the foraging segment, I stopped short of letting *"Morgan"* eat a mushroom that would've poisoned him. He wouldn't have died or anything, just a little total paralysis. Temporary, probably.

He'd had Kyle giggling all day, but *that* would've been something to laugh at.

Damn.

Missed opportunity.

In any case, by the time we got back to the main lodge, to sit down for the dinner my mother always hosted for each class, I was thoroughly pissed off.

And then I ended up directly across from Kyle and Morgan at the table.

That was exactly the motivation I needed to sit there and eat my food, finishing before the "official" end of class was over, and my duty to my job ran out. Otherwise, there was the substantial risk of me offending the hell out of my mother's residents, by setting free everything that was in my head.

I didn't want to hear mama's mouth about that.

So, I moved my ass along, intending to ease out while nobody was paying attention, but that plan was ruined by somebody calling my name from the front desk. I glanced back, laughing when I saw who it was.

"Should've known if mama was hosting dinner you wouldn't be far behind," I joked, pulling my hand back to smack Luke's in greeting before we pulled each other into a quick hug. "Where the hell you been, man?"

Luke shrugged. "Everywhere, dude. Seeing as much as I could. *Sampling* as much as I could if you get my drift."

"I do, and now I'm wondering what you're doing in Sugar Valley instead of out doing more of that?"

"Family shit," he answered, paired with a noticeable shift in his mood. "Granddad asked me to come back, and his health isn't in a place where I can..."

"Can't put it off anymore," I finished for him, when he didn't.

He nodded. "So you feel me."

"Always."

Even though Luke was a few years older than me, he and I

had always been tight. He was a city kid, who came to live with his grandparents here in Sugar Valley, which was... an adjustment. My mother tasked me with showing him around. To this day, I couldn't tell you what she'd intended for that to mean, but what it *actually* meant was, keeping him from getting his ass kicked at school.

For some reason, people who grew up in more urban areas thought street life made them tougher than "country folks".

It didn't, of course, which was a lesson Luke learned the hard way.

My peers and I had grown up doing the *dumbest* of dangerous shit – taunting and trapping bears and wolves, having gravel fights, jumping off the side of *Big Sugar* for fun, treating the river rocks like slip-n-slides.

The streets didn't mean shit to us.

Either you could fight, or you couldn't, and even if you could, that didn't mean somebody wasn't better than you. I watched Luke get his ass kicked a couple of times before my mother told *me* not to let it happen again. So I had to put *my* reputation on the line to protect him.

Luckily for both of us, Luke was a decent dude, so it didn't take much for him to be allowed in our circle.

I was almost nine, and he'd just turned twelve.

We'd been cool ever since, and now, twenty-five years later, he was damn near like a brother to me. We didn't talk often, but when we got together, depending on who you asked, it could be described as a problem.

In a good way.

"Your mom spotted me in the grocery store earlier, told me to come grab a bite. I got in a few hours ago, landed in Blackwood and drove down."

I nodded. "You may want to grab that plate before it's all gone, but tomorrow – me and you, the bar at *Maple*..."

"Consider that shit *done*," Luke agreed, extending his hand again. As we pulled back, something over my shoulder caught his eyes, making him squint. "Damn, I should've brought a lil' honey up to the mountains with me too," he mused.

I knew without looking that he was seeing Kyle, and Morgan was probably in her face. Dinner must've been over now, because a large crowd was leaving the dining room when I turned.

As suspected, Morgan had Kyle pulled off to the side.

I didn't have a chance to say anything about it before my mother rushed up to speak to Luke.

"I see you made it!" she gushed, pulling him into a hug which he returned.

"Come on, Ms. Regina you know if you tell me to come eat, I'm eating," he laughed. "But uhh... looks like I might be too late?"

Mama sucked her teeth, then lifted her hand to raise her finger, which she wagged at him. "Now you know me better than that, Luke Freeman!" she fussed. "You think I didn't put a little something aside for you?"

"Okay wait a minute, now," I interjected, frowning. "This dude ain't put a pinky toe in Sugar Valley in five years, but he gets a plate. The fire chief gets a plate. *Who else* is getting plates, but I can't?!"

"She's been feeding you for more than thirty-three years, Benny. Don't be selfish," Luke teased, as my mother gave him a proud grin.

"Come on baby," she told him. "And you too sweetie," she told Domino, who'd been resting at my feet. "I'm keeping her with me tonight, since you have such an early morning."

"Damn, you're taking my dog too?"

"You're tough baby, you'll survive," Mama called over her

shoulder, then turned to spark an animated conversation with Luke.

Shaking my head, I headed out the front door to the parking lot, but stopped when I noticed a familiar figure headed back to her cabin.

Kyle.

Seemingly struggling with the weight of her backpack after toting it around all day.

Just get in your truck and go home, fool.

That was the instruction common sense kept trying to beat into my head, but... that wasn't what happened. Instead of leaving it alone, minding my own business, I put my keys back into my pocket and jogged up to where she was. She was moving slow enough that it didn't take much, and from her reaction, she was too tired to argue much about it.

"I *don't* need your help," she said, stopping in the middle of the walkway to prop her now-empty hands on her hips.

"So you *don't* want me to carry it to your cabin for you?"

Lips pursed, she looked at me, then the bag, then down at her cabin, which was at least a few minutes' walk away. Finally, she shrugged.

"Fine. My shoulders are killing me anyway."

Silently, we walked a few moments, and then I asked, "Why didn't your new boyfriend Morgan walk you to your cabin? He doesn't seem like the type to let a woman walk in the dark alone."

"He isn't," she answered, with a little sigh. "I didn't want him getting the wrong idea though."

"The wrong idea?"

"Mmhm."

"And what might that be?" I asked, stepping aside for her to take the walkway to her cabin first.

She didn't say anything until we were on the porch, in front of the door, where she looked up to meet my gaze. "That walking me to my cabin might be an invitation inside."

"Oh damn, it's not?"

"I *really* don't like you," she declared, reaching for her bag, but I didn't let it go.

"Seriously... what's up?"

"What's up is that I'm tired, and all I want to do is take a long, hot shower, and sleep until noon tomorrow."

"A plan that would only be *enhanced* by a couple of orgasms."

Her eyebrow shot up. "A *couple?* Confident, aren't you?"

"Very. So why don't you quit playing and invite me inside?"

For a long moment, she just looked at me, with that pretty ass face set into an expression I couldn't decipher. After several seconds had passed, she let out a deep sigh, then pulled out her key and unlocked the door.

"Can you bring the bag in for me?"

She didn't wait for an answer.

She stepped in, holding the door open for me to follow, and then closed it behind me. I let the bag drop to the floor, and then... it was on.

As our lips connected, I didn't care about much else besides getting Kyle out of her clothes, and she seemed to be working from the same agenda. For a few minutes, we were a mess of clashing hands and clothes and curses until we were skin on skin.

I grabbed her by the thighs, lifting to carry her into the bedroom of the cabin.

"No!" she exclaimed, as I started to lower her. "I don't want the bed to smell like you after you leave."

A different man may have been offended by that – not me. Instead of the bed, I took her to the dresser, sweeping whatever was on top out of the way before I placed her down, then dropped my mouth to her neck.

She sucked in a breath, letting her head fall back to give me better access before I traveled lower, down to the stiff, dark peaks of her breasts.

Who the hell still smells like this after a day in the woods, I wondered, as I captured one of her nipples between my teeth, nipping hard enough to make her whimper, even though her hands at the back of my head told me she wanted me to stay exactly where I was. Her skin carried the subtle saltiness of dried sweat from the day's activities, but I was undeterred.

I wanted her, flat out, and wouldn't be swayed by a little natural seasoning. Spreading her legs apart, I started kissing lower, down her stomach, only to have her stop me once I'd gone past her belly button.

"Too intimate," she explained, in response to my questioning look.

"Fine."

Instead of arguing, I grabbed my dick, lining myself up and then plunging into her with one stroke that had her gasping and digging her nails into my shoulders.

"*Goddamn,*" I groaned, taking a second for myself. Kyle locked her legs around me, forcing me the *slightest* bit deeper in her pussy, but damn if it didn't feel like a whole other level. She felt different, *period.* Even better than before, hotter, softer, wetter.

How the hell is that even possible?

Damnit.

I answered the question in my head almost immediately after I'd asked it – the difference now was that there was no condom, which... honestly hadn't even crossed my mind.

Too late now.

"You're supposed to be a doctor, right? Tell me you aren't

burning."

"Kiss my ass," she hissed, whimpering a little as I shifted to the left. "Are you?!"

"Hell no. This isn't my norm."

"Mine either." Kyle's hands came to the back of my neck, urging me forward until our lips touched. "So shut up and fuck me."

"I'll try to pull out."

Her eyes widened. "Try?"

I shrugged. "Yeah, *try*. Pussy shouldn't be so good if you wanted a guarantee."

I never heard whatever she tried to say back – I kissed her, effectively silencing that noise as I pulled out and then stroked her again.

And again, and again, until the room was filled with the noise of the dresser rocking back and forth with every plunge. I kept my hands tight at her waist, digging into her soft flesh as I dug into her, as deep as I could get. With her head back, mouth wide open, Kyle was loud as hell, moaning and whimpering and cursing, and I was enjoying every second of it, noting the difference in reaction to every speed, angle, or depth I used to fill her up.

It wasn't until she slipped off the edge of the dresser that I decided to switch things up, letting her feet hit the floor before I turned her around to plunge in from behind.

That got her even louder.

I knew from my research as a horny teenager that these cabins had great soundproofing, so she could get as loud as she wanted, it wasn't a problem. I locked one arm around her waist to keep her where I wanted, and used the other hand to push between her legs, slipping through the moisture to play with her as I stroked, adding a new sound to the noise we were already making – the steady smack of skin on skin.

It seemed like no time before Kyle started coming unglued, practically melting on my dick as she came. I was right behind her, waiting until the *absolute* last possible minute to pull out, then trying and failing to keep it all contained, only to end up making a mess.

Worth it, if you asked me.

We ended up in the bathroom together, for a perfunctory clean-up in between long looks with tired eyes, both of us trying to gauge if the other was down for a second round.

Or... up to it.

I was exhausted though, and she had to be too, and we must have somehow come to a non-verbal agreement to call it a night, because I found myself flipping on the main light in the bedroom, to see exactly what we'd knocked off the dresser in our haste to get down to business.

"*Shit*," I muttered when I realized one casualty had been the decorative lamp that was in every cabin – I hadn't even heard it break at the time. Shattered pieces lay on top of the contents of a box that must've been on the dresser too, and lost its top on the way down.

I was stepping toward it to clean it up when Kyle peeked out of the closet, letting out a loud "*No!*" She rushed between me and the mess, closing a robe around her nude body as she looked at me with frantic eyes. "I'll clean it up myself. It's fine. You can go," she insisted, glancing at the pictures scattered on the floor once more before she looked back at me. "You got what you came for, right?"

Right.

I couldn't argue with that, so I didn't. I left her there and moved back into the main area to gather my own clothes and get dressed. I'd *never* been rushed out after sex before, so it was strange as hell to have Kyle hovering and pacing, arms crossed, in an apparent hurry to get me out of there.

Once I was dressed, she started prodding me, not even trying to cover it up.

"Goodnight," she said, opening the door for me with a flourish. I stepped out, then turned to make whatever smart comment came to mind, but she didn't give me a chance.

The door was closed and bolted before I opened my mouth.

"Damn," I said, to the closed door. "Goodnight to you too."

THE NEXT DAY, my mother had me up at the ass crack of dawn, helping around the lodge. Any other time, she pretended to have no computer literacy, but when it came to her to-do lists, there was a running document she kept, to update on the fly. She didn't even have to be awake to deliver my instructions – a fact she reminded me of with a note on her front door when I showed up.

That was why she'd taken Dom last night. So I wouldn't have to wake her up for an early morning drop-off.

This woman better be glad I love her, I mused, going back to the list after I'd finished pulling the weeds from the flower bed up front. Even though I complained... I didn't mind. I wasn't technically my mother's employee, but the fact that she used me like one anyway broke up some of the boredom of my *actual* job on the mountain.

I loved the woods, but it *could* get tedious sometimes.

Looking at the list, I noticed an item had been added in the last few minutes.

— *Replace broken lamp in Cabin 12.*
Kyle's cabin.
Yeah.
I was doing *that* next.
In the lodge's storage room, I grabbed a new lamp,

reminding myself to tease my mother about buying a whole pallet of them. There was an extra swagger in my step as I headed to Kyle's cabin, fully prepared to get on her goddamn nerves, only to have her not answer the door.

A quick look at the time said she'd probably gone to get breakfast.

Damn.

Since I already had the lamp, I used the maintenance keys to let myself inside. Before I moved any further than the door, I called out to announce myself in case she was there. When I didn't get an answer, I walked on into the bedroom.

It didn't bear any signs of the previous night's romp, except for the missing lamp. I took it out of the box and did the light assembly that was required before I put it in the empty space, then contorted myself to get the damn thing plugged up.

Done.

As I was standing up, my own stomach growled, letting me know it was time to look into a second breakfast for myself. I picked up the now-empty lamp box and turned, groaning when I felt the bump of me knocking into something, and then the *thud* of whatever it was hitting the ground.

The same box from last night.

All I intended to do was sweep the contents back inside and return it to the dresser – *that's all.* But, there had been a photo album inside, and it had fallen open, and I couldn't help the fact that I saw the damn pictures – they were right there in my face.

Kyle, as a much younger woman, cheesing for her life, and some guy beside her, smiling just as hard. There was a similar picture underneath that one, with space for a caption in between.

Happy Birthday.

They all said that.

Page after page, with them obviously getting older, sharing a birthday that was presumably on the same day. I turned another page, and my eyes bugged wide... about as wide as their smiles as they held up a positive pregnancy test.

And then, there was a baby.

A little girl, who appeared to be an even mix of her mother and father. A cute little happy family. The pictures were dated, one for every year until they abruptly stopped.

No picture for the last two years.

She's divorced.

There was nothing that *said* that, but it was easy to figure out. She'd come up here to find herself again, after smiling in pictures with ol' boy for... a lot of years, it seemed.

But it wasn't my business.

I snapped the book shut, sweeping everything back into the box and replacing the lid before I returned it to the dresser. I grabbed the lamp box and got my ass out of there before Kyle returned from wherever she was.

Well... I tried.

What *actually* happened was that when I stepped out, I found Kyle at the end of her walkway, with Morgan in her face.

Is she entertaining this motherfu—nope.

Nope.

I swallowed *that* shit, especially with what I knew now.

"Replaced the lamp for you," I told her, holding up the empty box as I approached. She was uncomfortable, and I could tell. Morgan, on the other hand, was oblivious.

"Thanks," she said, tucking a stray coil of hair behind her ear. "I appreciate it."

I grinned. "Any time I can be of service... ma'am."

Her eyes narrowed at me, which only made me grin harder as I headed back up toward the lodge, to finish my list.

I was ready to get back to the woods now.

CHAPTER SEVEN

I t had been a *long* time since I'd been to the doctor.

Of my own free will, at least.

Typically, I self-diagnosed my minor ailments and kept things pushing, but with me being in an unfamiliar environment, and having suffered a head trauma, I figured it was probably a good idea to honor the town doctor's request for a follow-up appointment.

Besides.

I wanted to meet the woman who kept Sugar Valley healthy.

It wasn't until I arrived that I realized Lilah Atwood's motives were similar – she quickly handled the medical aspects of the appointment up front, in favor of sitting down to talk in her office. And my head trauma was *not* the topic of interest.

"Did you know we've sent you patients before?" she asked, practically vibrating with excitement. Dr. Atwood was young – younger than me – and from a family line of doctors. Her father had been a doctor, and so had his mother, and so had her father, and so on. Lilah worked their local practice because her father had been forced to retire early, due to his own health. He still consulted at the office, but if you came in for an ache, pain, or cough, Lilah was your girl.

I nodded at her inquiry. "Well, not *you* specifically, but Blackwood Regional is the closest Level I Trauma Center, so I assumed. Hopefully you don't get too many patients who have to come to *me* though."

"No, thank goodness," she agreed. "Just a handful over the years. They usually come back patched up well. A few... never came back. Not alive, at least. But we usually can already tell they aren't... you know."

Yes.

I did.

Death wasn't a subject I particularly wanted to discuss, but it was apparent *she* wanted to. She'd been moving her chair steadily closer, and then leaned in when she couldn't move it anymore without being obvious.

"I'd sometimes see the name on the paperwork, and assumed you were a man, but imagine my surprise to find out you weren't just a woman, but a *Black* woman! And then you turned up in Sugar Valley, and I have so many questions, about everything, but mostly... How... how do you deal with it?" she asked, eyes sharply focused on my face. "I mean... by nature of what you do, you must... see more death than normal."

"I do," I agreed. Plenty of doctors had never seen death outside of their studies, but that was far from the case for me. By the time they made it to me, patients were facing a serious life or death emergency, and sometimes... it was simply too late. Sometimes the ailment or injury was too much. Sometimes the body failed, the equipment failed, *I* failed. My hands weren't fast enough, or I chose the left fork in the path when I should've chosen the right. I didn't want that to be true, but... sometimes it was.

I saved more lives than I lost, by a huge, *huge* margin. At a rate high enough that awards and useless praises got thrown around. But a high success rate didn't change the reality that trying your best to preserve a life, and still, ultimately, having to look at a clock and document the exact last moment of someone's life was...

Devastating.

"I sometimes wonder," Lilah spoke, then paused, like she was trying to choose her words carefully. "If I'm doing myself a disservice by staying here in Sugar Valley. Settling for the mundane." She laughed a bit. "But then, I have to visit the bedside of one of our elders in hospice, and it's like my heart is going to explode out of my chest. I wouldn't be able to handle anything more intense."

I shook my head. "It takes time. You're what... twenty-seven? Twenty-eight?"

"Twenty-seven," she nodded.

"I figured. Working at a big hospital sounds exciting, and it even looks that way on TV. You probably interned at Blackwood too, right?"

"Yeah."

I smiled, thinking of my own fresh-out-of-med-school days. "Nobody *starts* as a hotshot. You work up to it. Honestly, you have an edge, with getting to work a private practice. Avoid all the politics and red tape and *insane stress* of a big hospital. Get a spouse and have some kids, actually get to *see* them, if that's what you want to do..."

Lilah snorted. "Around *here*? Please. Nobody around here does anything for me."

"Damn, *nobody*?"

She tipped her head, and a dreamy sort of expression clouded her eyes. "Well... there is this *one* guy who I would... *God* I'd climb that man like a tree and never leave the bed. If I thought he'd stay there, that is."

"Ah, that *is* always the question, isn't it?" I laughed.

"Honestly it's not even a question with him – it's pretty much a guarantee. Whatever time God set aside for the making of Ben Wilburn, he spent it all making him impossibly fine, and didn't have time for personality. He's just so... *cantankerous.*"

My eyes were already wide, then went even wider in response to her word choice. It was perfect.

"That's unfortunate," I replied, keeping my tone light. "So the two of you... dated?"

Immediately, she shook her head. "Absolutely not. This is pure fantasy on my part, and always will be – I spent my summers home from college wrapped up with his cousin, Todd, who swears I'm going to be his wife someday. *When I stop playing,* according to him."

I laughed. "Okay, what's wrong with Todd?"

"On paper? Nothing," Lilah shrugged. "I just... don't have any butterflies? I know that sounds ridiculous, understand that marriage can't just be emotional, it must be practical as well, but... I want something amazing. Someone I'm thrilled to wake up to every day. I want... the great love of my life. If it's only going to happen once in a lifetime, I want *that* to be the person I call my husband."

Her words brought a deep ache to my chest, but a smile to my face, and I nodded. "Then that's what you should wait for."

Curiosity lit Lilah's eyes as they studied me, but something in *my* face must have given her pause, because whatever questions she wanted to ask, she held them back. I decided to capitalize on that, excusing myself before she got bold enough to pose them anyway.

Before that appointment, I'd been on the phone with Jude discussing recipes. Now that it was over, I headed to *Shaw's Grocery* to stock my cabin's refrigerator – something I'd meant to do since I arrived.

Every day, I'd found an excuse not to employ the simple task of cooking – something I'd avoided for years at this point. It wasn't because I didn't enjoy it... I loved cooking, and did some of my best thinking that way.

Which was, of course, the problem.

That, and my uncertainty of what feelings might be dredged up, by doing what was formerly an act of giving and service to someone else... for no one else.

It was a bit terrifying to think about.

But I wasn't supposed to be avoiding myself, or shunning the natural feelings I'd managed to suppress so far. Cooking was... a normal thing. It was unrealistic to sustain myself on pre-prepared meals, fast food, and ordering out.

This *had* to be done.

So I scolded myself for making something as simple as cooking dinner such a big deal, swallowed my trepidation, and grabbed a basket. Then, with trembling hands, I pulled out my grocery list... and shopped.

I took my time because I had nothing better to do. With every item, I looked at nutritional facts and checked prices and compared varieties and debated between sizes. I picked out the freshest meat, and meticulously checked the produce for any imperfections.

I was obsessing.

But obsessing was, at least, *something*.

"Excuse me?"

I looked up from my inspection of a spinach bundle to see a woman standing near me. She was wearing a *Shaw's Grocery* polo and a pleasant smile – more than the usual "customer service" expression.

"Yes?" I asked. "Can I help you?"

The woman's smile faded a bit, marred with uncertainty as

she stepped closer. "Are you... Kyle Desmond? *Doctor* Kyle Desmond?"

"I am," I told her, and the smile came back at full wattage. "I'm sorry, do we know each other?"

She nodded. "Well," she laughed a little, correcting herself. "I know *you*, but of course I can't expect you to remember me. You see so many patients, in that chaotic environment it has to be impossible."

My eyebrows raised, and then my eyes began a reflexive scan of her body, looking for surgery scars. "*Oh!* You're a former patient?"

Her lips pressed together, and she shook her head. "Uh... no, not me. My son, Devin... there was a fire at our house. A really, *really* bad fire, and he... you tried to save his life."

Immediately, my brain kicked into gear, scanning my memories for his name – it wasn't hard to bring him to mind. Severe burn injuries were... intense.

One of the hardest things to survive.

Vivid flashes played in my head – charred clothing, the acrid smell of smoke, the delicacy of his skin... the *extent* of his injuries, so bad that with every touch, every prod of an instrument, it was like his flesh was melting away.

Just as Lilah mentioned... I knew it as soon as I saw him.

But I tried anyway.

I knew now why I didn't remember this woman – *Donna Shaw, Manager,* according to the silver badge pinned to her chest. The pain in her eyes – the agony of losing a child – was still palpable now, in the grocery store. In the hospital that day, she would've been completely distraught.

I *had* to put her out of my head.

"You didn't have to be the one to tell us," Donna said, almost in a whisper as she grabbed my hand, threading her fingers through mine. "One of the nurses told me that later. That it didn't have to be you, but it was. And you... it was like it hurt you too. It wasn't clinical. He wasn't another number to you. Even his last moments mattered, and I... never got to tell you how I appreciated that. So... *thank you.*"

She pulled me into a hug, and she held on tight.

I hugged her back, giving her the comfort it seemed that she needed – another acting job, like the one she'd described from the hospital.

It *had* been clinical, for me.

Comforting the family was part of my job.

Devin Shaw had been wheeled in front of me at what should've been the absolute worst time of my life, but I was... firmly committed to not acknowledging it, to not feeling anything, to propping myself up as if nothing had happened.

It was the only way I preserved my will to live.

But it didn't make me any less of a fraud.

"She probably wasn't supposed to, but she – the nurse – told me a bit about your situation too. I don't even understand how you... were even upright at all, let alone working. But I'm glad you were."

I smiled at her when she pulled back, because it was what I was supposed to do.

"I'm glad to see you're doing well," I told her, earnestly. "But I'm so sorry there wasn't more I could do."

Donna shook her head. "You have nothing to apologize for, absolutely nothing. I was a mess, at the time. I couldn't tell you then what I'm telling you now. Sometimes I still am."

"Which is to be expected," I said. "You lost a child."

Retaking my hand, Donna nodded. "If you ever need to talk..." She slipped a card into my palm, then closed my fingers around it.

With one last smile, she headed off, and I turned the card over in my hand.

Shaw's Grocery
Donna Shaw, Store Manager.

A number I assumed was her personal cell was written underneath the printed words. I tucked it into my purse, along with the sudden overwhelming desire to leave my cart there in the store, and go home.

Only... I couldn't go *home*.

It was too familiar.

The textures, the décor, everything. The sounds were gone, and the smells were long faded, but my brain would sometimes try to fill those details in any way. An alarm that wasn't going off, a whiff of cologne, the rote memorization of notes.

I *had* to block it all out, had to tuck it away.

Either that, or let it consume me.

After a few deep breaths, I was okay to carry on. I finished my grocery list, checked out, and then headed back up to my lodge. Any appetite I'd had earlier was long gone, so I put everything away and then took a long shower before I climbed into the bed.

It was still afternoon, so the sun was high in the sky, easily streaming through the curtains even though they were pulled closed. My eyes landed on the box on the dresser. I purposely kept it there, in my site, to keep the contents near the front of my mind, even when I didn't want to.

Because I wasn't supposed to be backing down from it.

I'd have to call today a loss.

I got up, pulling down the room darkening shades before I got back in bed. This time, I faced the other way, away from the dresser, away from the box. Instead of letting my mind drift, I focused on clearing it completely.

I didn't want to think.

Didn't want to feel.

I just wanted to sleep.

I WAS COOKING when someone knocked at the door of the cabin.

It crossed my mind to ignore the uninvited visitor, at first. It had taken quite enough energy, as far as I was concerned, to get out of the bed at all. The decision to cook had taken even more.

I wasn't sure I had the energy for human interaction too.

But the knock sounded again, with the same casual cadence as before, and I decided to at least see who it was. My eyes widened in surprise when I glanced through the peephole, and I pulled the door open as Morgan was about to turn to leave.

"Uh... hi," I said, my face warming over his seemingly genuine happiness to see me.

"Hi yourself," he greeted, smiling. "Sorry to drop by like this, but you crossed my mind, and... we never exchanged numbers, so I couldn't shoot you a text."

I glanced over my shoulder at the pot bubbling on the stove. "It's fine. Um... can you step in? I need to check on that."

Without waiting for him to answer, I rushed to the stove, stirring to make sure the contents of the pot hadn't started sticking.

"It smells *amazing* in here, wow. What are you cooking?"

"Soup," I replied. "Chicken sausage, butternut squash, and kale." I looked at the pot, filled with much more soup than I could eat on my own – it hadn't occurred to me until halfway through that I should pare the recipe down. "Um... if you haven't had dinner, you're more than welcome to join me."

"Not gonna lie – I *have* had dinner, but it didn't smell like this, so I'm not going to turn a bowl down."

I laughed – which felt good. *Really, really good.* "Okay. Well... um, go ahead and have a seat, and I'll serve it up."

"Or, I can fix the drinks or something, right? Grab the silverware, napkins...?"

"Yeah, of course," I agreed. "Thank you."

"No, thank *you*. Like I said... you were already on my mind, so I'm happy to be invited into your space. Helping set the table is the least I can do."

IT ONLY TOOK a few minutes for us to get seated, with the hot soup in front of us. Morgan made me laugh no less than five times in that short span, including when he almost burned himself in his hurry to taste the soup.

"But it smells so *good*," he whined, when I scolded him about not letting it cool off.

"Okay, so... maybe you need a distraction until we can eat. You never did show me your artwork, and you promised."

He cocked a finger at me. "You're right. But my website is still down."

"I thought you said you were going to spend a few days out on your back porch with your laptop, fixing it?"

He scrunched his face. "See... What had happened was... I didn't do it. Didn't even try. I binge-watched two seasons of *Psyche* instead."

"Morgan!"

"At least I'm being honest!"

I laughed, shaking my head. "That's the spin you want to use?"

"Why do I feel like *yes* isn't the right answer for that?"

"Because it *isn't*," I giggled. "You claim to be an artist, but I've seen *no* art."

"That's why I'm up here, trying to create something. You can't fuss about it unless you're about to volunteer to be my muse."

My eyebrows lifted. "I'm *not* getting naked for you to paint me like one of your French girls."

"See?" he sucked his teeth. "I don't even paint French girls – I do performance art."

"What does that even mean?"

"It means, keeping up with your *Titanic* reference, I'm performing a scene where we *both* get on the door in the water, cause goddamnit there was room."

"There was *totally room*," I gushed, laughing.

"So you feel me?!"

"Absolutely."

Morgan grinned, then bit down on his lip as he shifted back in his chair. Then, he pulled his cell phone from his pocket.

"Okay, so... my site isn't up, right? But I *could* show you some of my stuff on social media. Not my preferred presentation, but I guess it's better than nothing."

"It's definitely better than nothing," I told him, nodding. "Let me see."

So he did.

He pulled up his page on Instagram and then handed me his phone, for me to scroll through. There were pictures and video clips of him in galleries displaying his work, time-lapses of his creative process, post after post of beautiful photo-realistic sketches and paintings. As I scrolled, I noticed that there was one woman who appeared often, either near Morgan at those galleries, or on his canvas.

She was gorgeous.

"Who is this?" I asked, instead of letting the question linger.

When he realized where I was pointing, his mood shifted – not a lot, but enough for me to notice. "Uh..." he pushed out a heavy sigh and shook his head. "Complicated."

"Understood," I told him, glancing through a few more posts. "Your work is... absolutely outstanding though. And, I think our soup is probably cool enough to eat without you burning your lip off."

"Hmmm?" he said, his mouth already full when I looked up. I laughed, then returned his phone so I could eat as well. "Listen – this tastes even better than it smells, which is bonkers to me."

"Cooking is honestly one of my favorite things. I haven't done it in a long time, so I was a little nervous about it, but... I'm thrilled with how it came out."

Morgan nodded. "You should be. But... why haven't you cooked in a while? You don't eat?"

"Of course I *eat*," I laughed. "We've had breakfast together, remember?"

"I do. Now answer the other question."

"What other question?"

He scoffed. "Come on, Kyle. Why haven't you cooked in a while?"

"That rhymes!"

"Seriously?"

"*Fiiine,*" I groaned. "It's... complicated."

For a moment, he stared at me, eyebrow raised, but then he nodded. "Understood."

From there, we finished off dinner and then he helped me clean the kitchen, which wasn't necessary, but was still appreciated.

I didn't want to be alone.

As much as I'd thrived on seclusion when loneliness had been my primary goal, now it only served as a source for direct, unfettered access to pain I didn't want to feel. Pain I was *supposed* to be feeling, yes, but... it was hard.

I couldn't stop contradicting myself.

Being on this mountain was supposed to hurt. I was supposed to ache, and sob, and scream, and let out everything

I'd been bottling up. And yet here I was, at every turn, swallowing my emotions. Taking the distractions and running with them, every chance I got.

I'd left my job, my patients, my *family*, to supposedly reconnect with myself. To rediscover my humanity. I was approaching two weeks here in Sugar Valley, but I wasn't sure I'd moved the needle at all on what I claimed to be here for.

Is this it? I wondered, sitting beside Morgan in front of the fire. This was where we'd settled, at some point, after the kitchen was clean. I didn't remember lighting the fire, didn't even know what the hell we were talking about, because my mind was on the pain I was trying to hide, but my mouth was running on auto-pilot.

A skill I'd honed to perfection.

But it wasn't fair to him.

So instead of dwelling in my thoughts, I mentally checked back into the conversation, listening as Morgan explained how he chose the subjects of his art.

"So you're telling me I can't just ask you to draw... an apple?" I asked, and he laughed.

"You *could*. And I could draw one for you, and it would be a perfectly good drawing of an apple. But that's... it. No depth, just art created on demand because somebody asked for it. I don't ever want to work like that."

"You don't take commissions?"

"I do," he nodded. "But it has to be a project I'm passionate about. Something I'm interested in, and actually *want* to do."

"What if it's a person?"

"You think you can't be passionate about a person?" Morgan asked. "Because I definitely beg to differ."

I didn't miss that he eased closer to me, but I didn't move back. "No, I'm not saying that. I'm asking what it takes. What are the qualifications?"

He shrugged. "Look in the mirror."

"What is that supposed to mean?"

"Did you already forget that I asked you to be my muse?"

"*Ohh*," I exclaimed. "Sorry. I get it now. You're interested in me and want to do me."

His eyes bugged wide. "Hold up, you're making me sound pretty brazen."

"I'm using the same words you did," I countered, laughing. "You said that your projects had to be something you were interested in and actually wanted to do. So if you're asking me to be your project..."

"I guess I walked right into that one, huh?" he chuckled.

"Yeah, you did."

"It's cool, I can handle it." He met my gaze. "Especially since... it's not like I can deny it anyway, I mean... I'm here."

I nodded. "You are."

"The question then, is... are you cool with that?"

"Cool with what?"

"With... me being interested in you."

"And wanting to do me?"

He laughed. "Yeah. That too."

I shook my head, but didn't break eye contact. "I'm not opposed. So long as you understand that *wanting* doesn't mean *getting*."

"No rush on my part, not for that. But... there is this one thing I've been wanting to do."

My eyebrows lifted. "What?"

"This."

I should've expected his lips, but I didn't, which made them a rather pleasant surprise. Full. Warm. Skilled.

Morgan raised a hand to my head, threading his fingers through the coils at the nape of my neck to keep me where he wanted me as his tongue slipped between my lips to caress mine. At first, I was just letting him kiss me, but after a moment, I kissed him back. His other hand came to my waist, gripping and pulling me into him before he wrapped his arm around me, holding me close.

It was a perfect, *perfect* kiss.

And yet... I was glad when he drew back.

Downright relieved when he kissed my cheek and then started the wind-down conversation to lead into us calling it a night.

It was just a kiss.

A *great* kiss with no pressure to take it further, and then... goodnight.

Thanks for dinner.

Yes, I *will* take some with me.

Mentally, I was in a daze of confusion, relying on my other faculties to lead me through walking Morgan to the door, accepting another soft kiss on the lips, and then closing and locking it behind him.

What the hell is wrong with you, Kyle?

I couldn't even attempt to answer that before my cell phone rang, the specific tone making me move a little faster to answer it. It was Jude, who I was supposed to call hours ago – a call that Morgan's presence had made me completely forget about.

"Sorry sis," I answered, laying back on the bed with the phone pressed to my ear. "I got caught up with an unexpected guest."

"Oooh," Jude gushed. "Big Dick Benny again?"

I rolled my eyes. "No. The other guy I told you about, Morgan."

"Oh, so you're up in the mountains being a *hoe* hoe. I approve."

"I am *not* being a hoe," I defended. "I mean... not like, on purpose."

"So you haven't got those draws yet?"

"*No*, Jude, I haven't *gotten Morgan's draws*. He did kiss me though. Which was... I don't know."

Jude groaned. "Ugh. Was he a bad kisser?"

"No."

"Okay... so what was the problem?"

"There wasn't a problem. Which... is kinda the problem."

"I'm not following you."

I pushed out a deep breath. "I just... I shouldn't be up here kissing anybody. Or screwing anybody. Or sitting by fires, or having breakfast, or any of that."

"Um... why the hell *not*? Kyle, you're an attractive, single woman. That stuff sounds like *exactly* what you should be doing."

"*Technically* single. And what I *should* be doing is thinking about my kid."

"Technically single is *still* single," Jude argued. "And you're completely bugging if you think anyone expects you to not have a life."

"It's not about what anybody else expects, it's about... what's appropriate."

"And you think enjoying yourself is inappropriate?"

"*Yes*," I countered. "I do. I didn't come here to... feel good. I came here to feel all the shit I've suppressed for two years, and it's not okay for me to just... *not*. I can delay it, fine. But I don't get to skip it. And that's what I should be focused on, not... cute potential romance. It's gross."

"Okay wow... so you're gonna go full self-flagellation on me, okay. I get it. Cool. I'll *never* understand why you have to do this to yourself, but fine. Rock on sis. You're a terrible person for coping with something horrific in the only way you could. It was *totally* a great idea to isolate yourself from your job and your family to go force yourself to be sad in the mountains."

"I'm about to hang up."

"Hang up then, bitch," Jude laughed. "If that's what you *feel*, do it! That's all I've been trying to get out of you for the past two years – for you to do what the fuck you felt like doing. Not what was expected, not what you thought you *should*. But what Kyle *wants* to do."

"You *just* mocked me for coming up to the mountains, which *is* what I wanted to do!"

"For wrong ass, unhealthy reasons!"

"That's not for *you* to decide!"

"I know!" For a second, Jude was quiet, and when she spoke again, her voice was choked. "I'm sorry, okay? I... I love you, more than damn near anything else in this world. It physically hurts me that you're beating yourself up for... everything. It wasn't your fault, Kyle. You're a victim too."

"Jude don't start that," I pleaded. "I'm not a victim."

"Fine, I'll rephrase. You're... it's like you have a cavity, right? And you pretend it's not there. You pretend, and you pretend, and then... one day you need a root canal, because of all the pretending."

"A dental analogy, baby sister? Really?"

Jude sucked her teeth. "I'm gonna use this knowledge, okay? Just roll with me. So you need a root canal. But... you don't have to do it without any anesthetic, to punish yourself. You don't deserve that. Maybe your injury wasn't physical, but you were *absolutely* wounded too."

"It's not the same."

"Isn't it?" Jude sighed. "Listen... Again, I'm sorry for being sarcastic, or whatever. I think the mountains are being good to you – a change of pace, a change of scenery, and... cute boys. You think because you skipped the tears and all that, that you... failed somehow. And if you need to let those tears out now, you need to cry, by all means do it, but... not by forcing pain onto yourself, sis. I don't want you to be numb anymore. I want you to feel, I want you to be human. I want you to cuss and cry if you stub your toe... but I don't want you sitting down with a hammer. You understand?"

"Despite your many, winding analogies..." I teased, "I think so. I'm just... I'm in limbo. I don't know what to do, and I don't know what I'm doing. Barely even know who I am. What I want. What makes me happy. I mean... I had it, but then it was just... *gone*. How the hell do you move on from that?"

"However you can."

After that, we did a much-needed change of subject.

Even with my nap earlier, I was so emotionally exhausted that I didn't stay on the phone much longer at all – a move that Jude honored.

After we hung up, I went out to the tiny back porch of the cabin, looking out over the mountain. The stars were out, and the moon was bright, illuminating the trees that lined the mountainside – the ones that extended up, rising with the mountain, and the ones that dipped into the valley.

Boundless and wild.

Uncultivated and unshackled.

If only I could use those kinds of words to describe **myself**.

Maybe that was part of the issue.

Maybe I was so uncomfortable because I couldn't recognize myself anymore. When I looked at myself over the last years, and looked at myself now, neither looked like the woman I was before.

And I wasn't sure *any* of those women were who I wanted to be *now*.

I wasn't sure I *could* be.

Right now... my only certainty was the surefire *un*certainty tomorrow would bring.

CHAPTER EIGHT

"C'mon girl!"

I whistled for Domino, urging her to follow me as I moved along the rough trail. Unsurprisingly, she ignored me, much more interested in chasing a squirrel who was having fun with their game. Suddenly, Dom yelped, pawing at her nose and looking to me for help. As I watched, the damn squirrel picked up a whirligig and launched it at my dog. Well – it tried. The shape of it made the maple seed spin, floating gently to the ground instead of the missile-like offense that had obviously been intended.

The first weapon must've been more successful.

"You coming now?" I asked Domino, and this time she followed, glancing back once more for her attacker. I rubbed her head, comforting her hurt feelings and trying not to laugh. She came out in these woods with me every day – at some point, she would realize that squirrels were assholes, not friends.

She found other ways to entertain herself while I "worked" – hiked along the back side of the public trail, scoping out potential dangers for the hikers who came through here every day that it was open. Signs of animal life getting too close, damage or disease to the vegetation, improperly disposed litter, hunters, etc. There was typically nothing to see, but as I approached the three-quarters point of the full mountain hike, a flash of color caught my attention, from the main trail.

A hiker was no cause for alarm, so I intended to move on about my business. Domino, however, always busy and looking for action, headed off through the trees to be nosy.

Which of course meant I had to follow.

"Putting your ass back on the leash," I muttered as I pushed my way into the clearing where she'd gone. When I didn't immediately see her, I made my way through an opening in the side of the mountain which led to a view of the waterfall.

And Kyle.

You'd think they were goddamn besties, the way Domino was tail-wagging and circling Kyle, who was good-natured enough to return the affection with a two-handed head rub, and words I wasn't close enough to hear. I stopped where I was for a moment, observing, until Kyle looked up – looking for me, probably – and grinned.

Has she ever smiled at me before?

"You look tired," I told her, because she did. I wasn't even *trying* to be rude that time, but the way her smile dropped and eyes rolled, that was how it was taken.

I wasn't lying though.

The ponytail... puff... thing... whatever... that had probably been neat when she left her cabin, was wrecked. She was sweating, there were streaks of dirt on her clothes, and as I stepped closer, the bags under her eyes came into even clearer focus.

She looked *exhausted*.

"Hiking a mountain tends to have that effect," she said, pulling a water bottle from the side of her bag. She opened the spout with her teeth, taking a long drink as she turned away from me, looking out over the waterfall. "I think I can see where I fell from here."

I chuckled. "Yeah, you made it quite a bit higher this time. You're turning around now, right?"

Her eyebrows lifted. "No, actually. I'm hiking to the summit today."

"You know what time it is?" I glanced at my watch, intending to make sure I wasn't mistaken about the time of day. I wasn't, but checking the time made me realize what today was, according to that photo album.

Kyle's birthday.

Only... I wasn't supposed to know that.

"You're probably another hour and a half to the peak, and then another three or four to get back down. It'll be dark before you make it back down."

She patted the side of her backpack. "Good thing I packed my light then. I'm prepared."

"I'm not trying to have to rescue your ass from this mountain in the dark. The hike is harder from here."

"I don't plan to need rescuing. I plan to make it to the top. So, unless you're coming with me, please step aside. I have a goal to reach."

I couldn't argue.

She was a grown ass woman, and the trail wasn't closed, so there was nothing I could do other than step aside like she'd asked. One last head scratch for Dom, and Kyle was off, continuing her path up the mountain.

Instead of dwelling on it, I grabbed Domino's leash from my own bag, hooking it to her collar with one end, and my belt with the other. I had my own shit to do.

I finished checking the trail and then headed back to my truck, parked at an inlet near the road. It was possible to drive up, not quite to the summit, but close enough, and that was the road I typically used for easy access. The road bisected what was a mix between private and public land, owned by the city. Mine was one of the few private properties on the side of the road that housed the trail up the mountain. The other side of the road was my responsibility too though.

Whether or not I wanted it to be.

So, I drove myself back down, pulling off the road to park in a small clearing. I didn't bother leashing Domino, because she never ventured far out here, in this area.

No one did.

In this part of the forest, there was a certain level of... eeriness. Before last year, it had been as full and lush as all the rest. Now, it was bleak.

Tall, scorched maples – the ones that hadn't been lost to the fire – sparsely decorated the terrain, the black trunks contrasting sharply against green new growth. The forest was trying to rebound, and the city tried to help by planting seedlings. In a few years, it would probably be fine.

For now, it looked like something out of a disaster movie. It wasn't visible from the main road, but once you came upon it, it took your breath away. Further out, there were healthy trees, wearing their thick foliage to show off. But then, in the middle, clear evidence that the area had been devastated.

All because of a cigarette butt.

A fire investigator researched it all afterward anyway, but it wasn't even necessary – some crying ass tourist came forward. It was protected property, that he wasn't even supposed to be in, let alone smoking in it, let alone *leaving behind* a half-lit cigarette butt, while we were experiencing a drought. Damn near an acre of forest, lost.

A life, lost.

Somehow, he ended up with what I considered a slap on the wrist.

I stopped at the property line – the invisible barrier separating what the city owned from what the former residents of the space in front of me claimed. The fire damage traveled on though, because it didn't care about man-made limits. Fire only cared about serving its primary function – destruction.

I could hear it, still. It haunted my dreams sometimes, the roar of fresh air being forced away from the flames, the sizzling and cracking of leaves and branches, the crashing and falling of trees. That decimation hadn't been confined to the forest either.

There used to be a house.

I stared at the concrete slab where it used to stand – almost the only evidence that it had ever been there. The winding driveway was nearly overgrown with grass and other vegetation, which was starting to creep over the slab as well. In a few years, there would be no sign of this. Not here, at least. The people affected by it would always remember.

Turning away, I moved to the nearest tree to conduct my real business – checking for damage. Even those that survived the fire weren't out of danger yet. They'd been weakened, which made them more susceptible to certain diseases and insects. Because this part of the forest was open to the public during hunting season, it was imperative that they were monitored as a potential safety hazard.

A job that fell to me.

I marked the trees as I walked, checking the bark and roots one by one, recording what I found and documenting with pictures. It was tedious, but necessary, even if my findings were the same as the last time I'd been tasked with this, which is what I thought until I came to the tree closest to the fire's point of origin.

It wasn't looking good.

The inner bark was dryer than the last time I checked it, and bark beetles had tunneled in, weakening the tree even more than it had been before. The leaves near the top were already turning colors, much too early – some of them appeared completely dry, brittle and brown.

Shit.

I put my weight against the tree, testing for movement as Dom circled it, barking at the leaves that came snowing down. I pulled out my phone to add more notes to my document, stopping when I heard a loud, air-splitting crack.

I frowned up at the tree, trying to see where the sound had come from as I backed away, getting out of the way in case it was about to come down. Only a few months had passed since I tested all these trees, but those beetles could ruin a healthy tree in a few months. These fire-damaged ones? *Weeks.*

Another cracked sounded, and this time I caught sight of the movement coming along with it. I called for Dom to come away, but she wasn't trying to hear it – she was much more interested in the steadily falling leaves.

And then, there was another crack, and I saw the branch coming down.

I was moving before I thought about it.

When she saw me running toward her, she took off in the other direction, thinking it was a damn game. With my eyes on her, I tripped over one of those maple saplings, falling and hitting the ground underneath the massive tree hard, just as the branch came crashing down.

At least *she* got away.

I cursed as the heavy branch landed on top of me, with my legs taking most of the hit. White hot pain shot through me, enough to take my breath away. Instead of trying to move, I laid back, talking myself through at least turning onto my back without vomiting from pain. Once I was there, I took a few deep breaths as Domino picked her way through the leaves, stopping to lick my face.

At first, I shooed her away, but that seemed to hurt her feelings.

"*Shit*," I muttered, wincing as a fresh round of pain whipped through me. "I love you girl, but you're gonna have to give me a few seconds, damn."

That seemed to satisfy her enough to stop trying to lick me – instead, she started barking at the branch, running circles around me. It was easily bigger than she was, and thick enough that it would have possibly killed her, which at least made my current situation seem worth it.

Maybe.

With ants, and beetles, and God knows what else crawling around on the forest floor, not to mention the larger wildlife, I couldn't stay on the ground. I took a deep, fortifying breath, then grabbed ahold of the branch to lift it, knowing I only needed enough space to slide my legs out.

I managed to get myself into a seated position, then strained to lift the massive limb. Once I had it up, I started to ease out, and had already begun congratulating myself when the part of the branch I was holding crumbled in my hands, slipping out of my grip.

The bulk of the tree limb fell again.

There was no flash of white-hot pain this time.

This time, I saw black.

MY LEGS WERE SCREAMING.

My back was screaming.

My feet were screaming.

But still.

I'd promised myself I would complete this hike today, because I was *supposed* to finish this hike today.

It was in my plans.

Our plans.

I remembered, vividly, when Jay and I said we'd do it. With his fear of heights, it had been more of a dare than anything else, but we'd added it to our shared family calendar for this day, for this year.

I'd forgotten, until I got the calendar notification on my phone.

It felt like divine providence that I was here.

It *also* felt like a knife in my chest, but I didn't let that hinder my newfound determination to conquer Sugar Leaf mountain, *today*.

My legs and back and feet could make all the noise they wanted – I had one more peak to climb, and I'd be there, and I hoped the view would be as worth it as everyone claimed.

It... *was*.

It so, *so* was.

In my research, I'd discovered that Sugar Leaf mountain had been a volcano, a very, *very* long time ago. The only real evidence of that now was the lake – created when the volcano collapsed on itself, forming a vast crater that collected rain or snow, depending on the season. When there was enough precipitation for the water to rise above a certain point, it ran off the side of the mountain – feeding Sugar Leaf Falls.

It was *gorgeous*.

The water was crystal clear and calm, reflecting the mountainous crater and trees around it. There was no one else here – probably due to the time of day, or the season, or more divine providence. Whatever it was, I was grateful for the solitude, and took a seat, staring as the sky reflected over Sweet Water Lake's turned from pure blue to bands of royal purples and oranges and deep golds, as the sun began to sink.

And I cried.

I couldn't explain why.

Didn't even care to understand it.

It felt good, so I let it all go, until the steadily fading light reminded me that I had to get back down the mountain.

Just like Ben had warned, it was dark before I was even halfway down.

By this point, weeks after my first arrival in Sugar Valley, I'd hiked the lower part of the mountain so many times that I was a bit of a pro at it, and I made it with no issue. It wasn't until I was back on the lodge property that I pulled out my phone, responding to a few late *happy birthday* texts from the coworkers, friends, and family I wasn't close enough to to indulge a phone call that morning before my hike.

And then, there was one from Morgan.

He didn't know what today was, by design. I needed to spend this day *my* way, unconcerned about suppressing unpredictable reactions to the well-wishes of virtual strangers. I had no idea how I was going to feel from one moment to the next – no idea if two little well-meaning words would make me break down in the middle of the grocery store.

So, I kept it to myself.

"Have dinner with me after your solo hike? – Morgan."

I sighed.

Maybe it would've been an excellent way to end the day, on a different day.

Not this one.

"Sorry, just now seeing this, and I'm exhausted. Rain check?"

He'd sent that text hours ago, so I hoped I hadn't insulted him with the late response, but as usual, he was cool.

"No problem. How was the view? You take any pictures? – Morgan."

I grinned. *"Nope. You have to see it for yourself."*

"Maybe we can hike it together, before either of us leaves... - Morgan."

That made me swallow, hard.

I could play it off for now, but honestly couldn't see myself making that hike with anyone except the man I'd planned to do it with. And since that wasn't happening...

"We'll see. Maybe I'll see you around tomorrow?"

I tucked the phone away to unlock the door to my lodge, leaving my heavy backpack by the door. My first order of business was the longest, hottest shower I could stand, followed up with thick, fuzzy socks, leggings, and an oversized hoodie from my alma mater.

Starving wasn't a strong enough word to describe my level of hunger, but I had a solution on deck for that. Right on the counter was a bakery box I'd removed from the fridge before I left for my hike, so that the small cake inside would be the perfect temperature by the time I was ready for it.

With a lump in my throat, I moved it to the dining table.

My hands were trembling as I opened the box, revealing the perfect cake – a layer of vanilla, a layer of chocolate, and plenty of cream cheese frosting.

The cake we always got.

Carefully, I placed three candles on top, then lit them.

"Oh, *God*," I muttered to myself, shaking my head as I tried to blink back a fresh round of tears. I didn't want to let them fall, didn't want a repeat of the time I'd spent sobbing up on the mountain.

Unbidden, *"It's My Party"* popped into my head, and I let a stuttering laugh break from my lips as those tears fell. I sobbed my way through the saddest, sorriest birthday song, then closed my eyes.

"I wish I felt something other than this pain today."

And then I blew.

I opened my eyes to three trails of smoke wafting from the extinguished candles, but no sudden rush of euphoria.

"What a fucking scam," I mumbled, picking up the fork I'd brought to the table with me and jabbing it into the cake, collecting a considerable chunk to shove into my mouth. I was like that for several minutes, gorging myself with – delicious – cake, until I heard a strange sound that made me look in the direction of the door.

Was there... was something *scratching?*

Just when I was ready to place a phone call to lodge security, there was a sharp bark, and the scratching continued. Strangely enough... I felt like I recognized the bark, so I got up, pulling the door open to find Domino on the other side.

But no Ben.

I peeked out, figuring he had to be close by, but I didn't see him. Stepping out onto the porch, I looked up and down the street but still didn't spot him, which was... *odd.*

Domino was excited about something, jumping around and barking and tugging at my sweatshirt with her teeth. Trying to get me to... follow her?

"Hey," I said, rubbing her head, to urge her to calm down. "Is something wrong? Is Ben okay?"

Instead of answering – *obviously* – she merely pulled at me harder. I thought about it for a few seconds, then grabbed my hiking boots from beside the door and slipped them on, then my flashlight and phone.

"Okay. Fine. What are you trying to show me?"

She was excited that I'd taken whatever hints she was trying to throw out, tail wagging as she darted off toward the road. Cautiously, I followed, moving fast to keep up with her frenzied, just-under-a-run pace, for nearly half a mile.

My chest got tight when I spotted Ben's truck, parked in a little clearing just off the road.

Domino urged me forward, barking and whining to keep me moving. Through the dense, old-growth maples that the whole area was named for, until we reached a huge area that... looked like something from a horror movie.

Gone were most of the tall, majestic trees – the few that were left appeared charred in the wide flashlight beam. This wasn't a place I wanted to stay any longer than I had to, so I cast the light around me, searching for Domino in the dense underbrush.

It didn't take long to spot her bright white fur.

I gasped when I approached her and saw Ben sprawled on the ground, eyes closed. There was a huge branch, damn near half the thickness of a telephone pole over his legs, and my stomach lurched over the awkward twist of one of his ankles.

It would be a miracle if it weren't broken.

"Ben. *Ben*," I urged, kneeling beside him to shake his shoulder. When he didn't respond, I checked for a pulse – to my relief, he still had one. But he really, *really* needed to wake up. At night, the mountain air was *cold*.

Realizing what I was trying to do, Domino chipped in,

licking Ben's face as I tried to rouse him. After a few moments, Ben groaned, which sent relief rushing through my chest. A few more licks, and his eyes opened, squinting and searching around in a daze before they landed on me. His gaze rested on my face, and for a moment I was scared – did he have a concussion? Did he hit his head? Did he remember anything?

"*Ah, fuck.* It's you," he mumbled, and I grinned.

Yeah.

He remembered.

"Yeah, it's me," I told him, shining my flashlight in his eyes to check his pupils. "*My, my my,* how the tables have turned. Your pupil response is good. Where all are you in pain?" I moved the light to his head, looking for visible injuries.

"I'm not in pain anywhere," he answered, making me frown.

I pointed my light toward his legs, making sure I'd seen what I thought I had. "That's not possible. Not with your ankle turned that way. You can drop the tough shit."

"Nobody is being *tough,*" he countered. "I'm telling you... I don't feel it. I *can't* feel it."

"Oh. Okay."

I didn't let any panic creep into my voice, but that... wasn't good.

At all.

"Do you remember any other injuries, besides the leg? Nothing to your back, nothing to your head?"

"No."

"And you can feel this?" I asked, gently running my nails over his palm. Once I got an affirmative answer there, I checked his other hand, then slid a hand underneath to check his spine, even though he insisted it wasn't necessary.

Then I had to address his legs.

"Hey, I have to get this tree limb off of you, okay?"

CHRISTINA C JONES

"*Hold up!* Just... call somebody. Where is my phone?"

I shook my head as I used the light to determine my best method. "I don't know where your phone is, but if you can't feel that ankle, I need to look at it, *now*."

"How are you going to lift that branch?!"

My eyes widened, and I propped the flashlight on the ground so that it was shining where I needed it. "Uh... with my hands and arms?"

"There's no way you're getting that thing up."

I sucked my teeth, glaring at him even though he probably couldn't see me. "I've picked up *patients* before, when necessary. I am quite sure I've got this."

I did.

The branch was heavy, so I understood his concern, but it was also in my way, which meant it was moving. Once I had it clear of his feet, I dropped it off to the side, then immediately grabbed my flashlight and got down to business, unlacing his hiking boot.

His foot and ankle were so badly swollen I could barely get it, or his sock, off.

It was necessary though.

I pressed a finger against the bottom of his foot, concerned by how quickly the spot turned pale. When I released it, it took way too long for the color to come back, which meant there was an issue with his blood flow.

Shit.

"Do you feel this?" I asked, running my nails over his foot the same way I'd done with his palm. When the answer was no, that he still didn't feel *anything*, I pushed out a deep breath. I grabbed his foot with both hands, my frown growing even deeper when I realized his skin wasn't nearly as warm as it should be. I braced my feet on the forest floor on either side of his leg, and then pulled, as hard as I could before turning his foot back in the direction it was supposed to be set.

"WHAT THE FUCK?!"

Everything and everybody between the woods and the town probably heard that, but I smiled at his exclamation.

It was a good thing.

"What the hell is *wrong with you?*" Ben growled, as I shined the light in his face again. "Man, get away from me," he told Dom, who was back to licking his face. "Out of all people you brought *her?!*"

"Because *she* recognizes that I'm the most qualified medical professional for miles and miles," I teased. "Is there a first aid kit in your truck?"

"Yes."

"Does it have a traction splint in it? Or do you have hiking poles, anything I can use?"

"The kit has a splint," he groaned, trying to pull himself into a seated position, which I immediately put a stop to.

"Please, stay flat for now," I urged. "Give me your keys. I'll be right back."

Reluctantly, he fished his keys off the ring on his belt, and I took off at a sprint to get back to his truck. The first aid kit was precisely where he said it would be, and I started to grab it, but thought better of it.

I got in the truck and turned it on.

I couldn't pull all the way to where Ben was, but there was a big enough space to get closer, which would be critical to getting him to the vehicle.

I could use an official emergency response right now.

Sugar Valley wasn't big enough to have its own hospital, but there was an EMT I *could* call. But I knew enough about how the small town EMT worked – the closest thing to a critical care doctor for thirty miles. They were overworked and underpaid, and probably trying to sleep right now.

I could do this myself.

So I *would*.

I jogged back to where Ben was with the big first aid kit in hand, making quick work of getting his leg splinted. The good news was that whatever blood flow had been hindered by the awkward position of his ankle was returning. The bad news was that with restored feeling, there was returned pain, and I still had to get him in the truck.

We will get this worked out.

We had to.

Getting him onto his feet was difficult, but we managed, with him using the hiking poles as makeshift crutches to aid the short trip to the truck. The next hurdle was maneuvering him into the passenger seat, which we accomplished with no shortage of cursing. Once he was in, I stepped up to buckle him into his seatbelt, which was the source of a fresh round of complaining.

"I *could've* called somebody and left your ass out there alone to wait," I told him, looking him right in the face. "I understand that you're in a high level of pain and discomfort right now, but... damn, you haven't even said *thank you*. So the least you can do is shut the hell up."

Without waiting for a response, I stepped down, closing the passenger side door. I let Domino in on the driver's side before I climbed in myself, grateful for the buffer between us so I wouldn't have to look at Ben as I guided the truck back out to the clearing in reverse.

I stopped the truck, letting it idle before I pulled onto the road. "So, you have options here. I can take you to the hospital to get treated, which is a thirty- or forty-minute drive," I explained, as I turned the heat on, to warm him up. Domino had already climbed into his lap to start the process. "Or... I can wake up Lilah Atwood, to get access to her office, and treat you myself."

"I don't need surgery."

"Surgery isn't the only thing I'm capable of doing though," I explained. "I think your ankle is broken. You need an x-ray, which the office has, and either a boot, or a cast – both of which I assume the office here can accommodate. But you must decide now, because you need that x-ray as soon as possible. And probably something for the pain."

"I didn't *have* any pain, until you snatched my foot in a goddamn circle," he muttered.

"Well excuse the hell out of me for not wanting this conversation to be about an amputation, because your tissue had died from lack of blood flow. *My bad.*"

Ben pushed out a deep breath. "Just... take me to Doc's office. I have keys."

I raised an eyebrow as I shifted the truck back into gear, to start moving. "Oh really? Something going on between you and the doctor?"

"Nah. I have keys for all the major buildings in town, in case of an emergency."

"Oh. I guess that makes sense."

It only took a few minutes to make it to the office, where I offered to grab a wheelchair to help Ben inside. He refused, which made the transition take even longer, but... it wasn't *my* leg. I wasn't about to argue.

Domino stayed by the waiting room door, while I got Ben settled on an exam table, then scrubbed myself from fingers to elbows before donning gloves. I was familiar enough with the portable x-ray to get the images I needed and pull them up on the screen to show Ben what was going on.

"So, it's definitely broken," I explained, using a stylus to highlight the fracture. "This area right here, the medial malleolus – the end of your tibia, essentially. You see the split there? It's a simple fracture, which is good, but I'm going to have to reset it. I got it mostly back in place out in the woods, but I didn't take it far enough. I need to correct that, before we can do anything else."

"You mean that snatching shit again? *Hell* no!"

I shook my head. "I understand that it's painful, but if you want it to heal properly, this is something that *has* to be done. I can give you a hematoma block – it's a local anesthetic, which will give you some relief so you can rest too."

He sighed. "Fine. Just... do whatever you need to do, so I can get the hell out of here."

"Okay," I nodded. "I'll get you taken care of."

It took a few minutes to gather supplies, but then I was back, ready to move forward with the procedure. I used the x-ray image to determine the best placement for the anesthetic, cleaning the area before I administered it.

"So... what in the world happened out there?" I asked, studying the x-ray images again to determine exactly where I needed to reset the bone. Blackwood Regional had the technology for me to see the bone while I was working with it. Here, I was going to have to work it out on my own.

"I was checking the health of the trees. That one... wasn't healthy. I tripped, trying to save my damn dog, a tree limb fell on me. The end."

"The health of the trees... what happened out there?"

"Fire."

I raised an eyebrow. "Well. No one can accuse you of being too talkative, now can they?"

When he just looked at me, and didn't say more, I took the hint – he didn't want to talk about it. Instead of forcing the conversation, I got to work, cutting off his pants leg so that there was nothing in my way. I offered an oral painkiller, for when that anesthetic wore off – because it *would* wear off, and so would the numbness he'd experienced from the lack of blood flow.

"Trust me," I urged. "You *want* to take a painkiller for it."

He took it.

And then I reset his ankle.

His reaction was much different this time, thanks to the local anesthetic. Instead of a cast, I got him fitted in an immobilizing boot, which I figured would work better with Ben's lifestyle – even though he was going to have to take it easy for at least a few weeks. The boot was also better for me – quicker, less messy – and gave plenty of room for him to get a second opinion if he wanted, without a bulky plaster cast in the way.

"Okay, you're all set," I told him, and I put everything back as I'd found it. "We can get you out of here. You're probably exhausted."

"Yes, I am," he admitted. "I'll drop you off at the lodge."

I frowned as he put his weight onto the crutches I'd handed him. "You'll do *what*? Ben, you can't drive right now – your ankle is broken."

"Yeah, the left. I do all the important shit with my right."

"That's *really* not the point," I countered. "Besides – you took a painkiller which should be kicking in soon. I can't risk you falling asleep at the wheel. You'll come to the lodge with me."

He sucked his teeth. "Says *who*?"

"Says *me*. Your doctor, for right now at least. And you *will* follow the doctor's orders. It's not negotiable."

"I don't know who you think you—"

"Just bring your ass, please," I interrupted, shaking my head. "You're not the only one who is exhausted, and this is not an argument you're going to win. Just come on."

He huffed and puffed about it, but he got his ass in the truck – the *passenger* side – for me to drive up to the lodge.

I helped him inside, then made him sit down at the kitchen table, instead of crashing onto the couch like he wanted. I found two large plastic bowls in the kitchen, filling one with clean water, and used my body wash to make the other soapy, and grabbed a few towels.

"What are you doing?" he asked, eyes half-open as I unstrapped his watch and took it off, then attempted the same with his shirt.

"At the hospital, it would be called a sponge bath, which you need, after being on the forest floor for God knows how long. I saw a few ants. We need to get them off you."

After that explanation, he let me pull off his shirt, and closed his eyes as I ran the hot towel over his skin.

"You expect me to believe you do this for your patients?"

I chuckled a little. "No, not at all. Nurses would do this part, bless their souls. I don't get to interact with patients in this way anymore. No quiet moments."

"That's what you wanted, right? To be a hotshot surgeon?"

"I don't know about all that." I frowned at the obvious, raised insect bites on his skin, which had gone unnoticed because of the higher priority of dealing with his ankle. He probably didn't even feel them yet, but would tomorrow. I got up, retrieving a tube of hydrocortisone to treat everywhere I saw one of the raised welts. "I'm going to have to cut your pants off," I told him. "You can keep your boxers on I guess, but I need to check everywhere."

"I feel like you're trying to get me naked, Dr. Desmond."

"You wish," I told him. "Do you have any extra clothes, in your truck?"

He nodded. "Yeah. There's a bag. But... hey... what's up with the birthday cake?"

I froze, then followed his eyes to the half-eaten cake on the table, those candles still standing high in the middle. "I... um..."

"Do you mind?" he asked, picking up the fork I'd left there without waiting for an answer. "I'm starving."

"Oh! Uh... yeah, that's fine. Eat as much as you want."

While he tucked into the cake, I used it as an opportunity to step away, under the guise of getting water for him. This was turning out to be far different from the day I'd expected to have, but that... wasn't necessarily a complaint.

The distraction was welcomed.

"Um, did you ever find your phone?" I asked, as I came back to the table. "Do you need to call someone, tell them you're safe?"

He shook his head, mouth full of cake as he answered. "All my people are used to me tapping out. They know I'll get to them when I'm in the mood for it. My lack of communication doesn't raise alarms."

Sounds familiar.

"Perils of being a loner, huh?" I told him, as I used the scissors I'd grabbed on the way back to remove his pants. "If that wasn't your norm, someone might have spotted you sooner."

He shrugged, looking a little *too* comfortable with me kneeling in front of him, between his legs. "Either way, it worked out – I'm not out there anymore. I still don't know why the hell Dom came to you instead of... my mother. Or Luke."

"Maybe they were busy, or didn't answer? I'm going to assume Luke is an adult, and so is your mother. Maybe they were asleep, or... engaged in adult activity. *I* wouldn't have stopped taking backshots to answer the door for a dog."

"Why would you even imply that my mother does such things?"

I laughed. "Because she's an attractive, healthy, vibrant

woman. She probably *does*. Isn't the fire chief like her boyfriend or something?"

Based on the look he gave me, that must have been a sore point, so I let it go, in favor of giggling like a child as I checked–*thoroughly* – inside his boxer briefs for any more insect bites.

He wasn't amused by *that* either.

He was, however, barely awake by the time I finished wiping him down, making sure he wasn't taking any of the forest into my bed with him. Domino circled us as I helped him up and onto the crutches again, for the trip to the bedroom. When we maneuvered him down to the bed, his eyes weren't even open, but that didn't stop him from looping his arm around me, bringing me down with him.

"Dr. Desmond," he slurred, eyes still closed. "You know what would help me feel a *lot* better?"

"Absolutely not," I answered, shaking my head as I wriggled out of his hold, being careful not to bump his ankle. "You're in no state to consent, for one. And for two... it would be a breach of trust between doctor and patient."

Somehow, he found the energy to sit up, grabbing my wrist to pull me closer. "Just... sit on my face real quick. For like two minutes, come on."

"You are *so* high right now," I laughed. "Go to sleep."

He groaned. "Fine. *Fine.*" He let me go, and laid back, eyes closed again.

I turned to walk away, to go clean up the mess in the kitchen before I took my own shower.

"Hey!" he called out again, and I turned to find him still sprawled across the bed, but looking at me. "Thank you. For all of this. My bad for not saying it sooner."

My eyebrows lifted.

Damn.

He only needs half a painkiller moving forward.

"You're welcome," I told him, giving him a nod before I flipped off the light and stepped out.

Domino kept me company while I handled the kitchen. It wasn't until I retrieved my phone from my back pocket, where it had been since I followed her out to find Ben, that I realized the time.

Past midnight.

Which meant my birthday was over.

I'd survived.

Domino nudged my hand, and when I gave her my attention, I realized she had one of the birthday candles hanging from her mouth. Once I took it from her, she walked off, curling up on the rug while I stood there looking at the candle, dumbfounded.

Maybe that whole *birthday wish* thing wasn't a scam after all.

CHAPTER NINE

*S*hit!

My eyes popped open at the sound of the smoke detector going off. What would've been panic was instead annoyance. I already knew there was no fire, but acrid smoke filled my nostrils as I pulled myself up, grabbing my crutches to hobble to the kitchen.

I'd fallen asleep with my dinner still in the oven.

Hours ago, according to the clock.

Usually, Domino would've raised the alarm about it, well before it had gotten to a point of the smoke detectors. Today, however, she was with my mother – despite my insistence I could take care of her.

She wanted to make sure her "baby" was okay.

Meaning Domino, not *me*.

I groaned as I pulled the chicken out of the oven. The thighs I'd marinated all morning looked more like charcoal briquets than anything edible now, thanks to my sudden change in routine. I was used to being up and about, high mobility. The fact that I wasn't back at a hundred percent a whole *week* after this damn ankle fracture was pissing me off.

And making me lazy.

Time I usually would have spent out in the woods had been wasted killing brain cells in front of the TV. The lack of activity made me sluggish, and paired with the intense boredom, most of what I spent my time doing was sleeping.

Which was why I had nothing for dinner now.

I started the slow process of getting around the house to open my windows and doors to let the smoke out. Once that was done, I dumped the chicken and set up the pan to soak, then foraged my cabinets until I found a box of cereal.

I filled half of a mixing bowl, drowned it all in milk, plopped a spoon in it, then made the awkward ass trip back to the couch. I'd just put a spoonful in my mouth when I heard a light knock at the front door.

"*Hello?*" I immediately recognized Kyle's cautious voice. "Ben, are you here? Are you okay?"

The creak of the floors told me she'd stepped inside – I hadn't closed the doors or windows yet – and I was still debating whether I was getting up or not when her head peeked around the corner.

"*Oh.* There you are," she said, sounding relieved as she stepped fully into view, holding a Tupperware container.

Goddamn she looks good.

I'd never understood the logic of wearing shorts with a sweater, but I highly approved of her thighs on full display in fringy, cut-off jeans. The sweater was hanging off her shoulder, showing skin *there* too, enough to make me wonder if a bra was even part of the equation.

"It looks like I might be right on time to offer something better than cereal for dinner," she explained, holding up the container in her hands.

My eyebrows rose. "You're about to get naked?"

"*No,*" she fussed, rolling her eyes. "Why would I do that?"

"Because you feel bad for putting this boot on me."

"Because your ankle is broken."

"So you say. What's in the dish?"

"So *I* say?" She shook her head. "So your *x-rays* say." Instead of answering my question about the dish, she took the lid off it and headed my way, the smell reaching me before she did. Suddenly, the cereal seemed even less appetizing than it already was.

I wanted whatever she had in her hands.

She lowered it, showing me roasted brussels sprouts, mashed potatoes that looked homemade, and chicken and mushrooms in some kind of sauce.

"It's chicken marsala," she explained. "You can't get around like you normally might. I figured you might be hungry."

My stomach rumbled.

The food in that dish looked and smelled amazing, but Kyle and I weren't exactly friends – life-saving adventures aside.

"How do I know this isn't laced with something," I asked, working my way up from the couch as she walked into my kitchen. "You could be trying to kill me."

"If I wanted to kill you, I would *not* waste good food to do it. Not when there are so many better ways."

"Is that supposed to be comforting?"

"I wasn't going for comfort. I was speaking the truth." She moved to the sink to wash her hands, stopping when she noticed the burned-out pan in the sink. "You tried to cook something?"

"Tried, yeah."

She laughed. "Mmmhmm. Have a seat."

I took a seat at the counter as she took down plates and glasses, and got forks for both of us. Even though it took her a bit of searching, she didn't ask questions, so I wasn't compelled to point anything out.

Besides, I liked the view.

"How do I even know you can cook?" I asked, as she began making plates.

Kyle looked up, wearing a smirk. "You don't... but I *can*. And I can prove it," she added, sliding the plate across the counter to me. She extended a fork, and I took it, ready – and willing – to latch onto any reason to roast her into oblivion.

There were none.

There was only tender, flavorful chicken, buttery mushrooms and savory sauce. Crispy edged brussels sprouts. Perfectly seasoned, perfectly textured mashed potatoes.

Goddamn, I thought, closing my eyes as I chewed another forkful.

"So...?" Kyle asked, watching me. She still hadn't taken her own first bite.

I shrugged, easily pulling another piece of chicken away with my fork. "It's aiight."

Immediately, she laughed, then lifted her fork to her plate. "If I speak *Ben* as well as I think I do, that *must* mean it's amazing. Am I right?"

"I'm eating it. Can't you be happy with that?"

"Because the privilege of feeding you should make my time at the stove worth it?"

"So you aren't as dimwitted as I thought you were, huh?"

I grinned as she flipped me off, her mouth too full of food for a verbal response. When she did speak, it wasn't to whine about what I'd said to her.

"I had a bottle of wine I should've brought. Really would've set these flavors off," she mused, regarding her plate. "And I *know* you don't have any."

"You're right, I don't – I *do* have local bourbon though."

She raised an eyebrow. "And... ingredients for an old-fashioned?"

"*Hell* no. You drink my liquor, you've gotta drink it straight up."

"Why doesn't that surprise me?"

I shrugged, chewing another mouthful of chicken before I answered. "You claimed to know me, so..."

"I didn't claim to know you, I said I spoke your language."

"Same difference."

"*Is it* though?" she teased, with a smirk. "Where is this bourbon?"

I pointed it out, and then watched her as she retrieved it, wondering how the hell – *why the hell* – I was so comfortable with this woman in my home. Sure, the fact that she was beautiful had plenty to do with it – it was hard *not* to look at her when she turned back to the counter with the bourbon and two glasses in her hand. Those big, pretty brown eyes lifted to meet mine before she smirked and cracked the bottle open, pouring a shot for both of us.

She slid mine across the counter and then raised hers. "To these bomb ass brussels sprouts," she said, and.... Hell, I could drink to that, so I did, draining the shot.

"What's the real reason you came up here with dinner?" I asked, apparently catching her off guard, from the way she sputtered and coughed.

"Excuse me?"

"What are you doing here? I don't believe for a second you decided to fix me dinner out of the kindness of your heart."

Her gaze dropped for several moments, and then she sighed. "Fine. I... haven't mastered cooking for myself yet. I'm used to cooking for a family, so when I get to the kitchen, that's what my hands do. I cooked too much. Didn't want it to go to waste."

"What about your little boyfriend?" I asked, digging into the topic since it seemed to make her uncomfortable. "*Morgan.* I'm sure he would've loved to find you at his door."

She laughed. "Yeah, so am I. Morgan is sweet. *Really* sweet."

"So why are you *here*?" I raised my hands. "You definitely seem like the type to marry the nice, sweet guy, have his babies, live in a cute house, all that. None of that shit is *here*, not in this house."

"Then you've answered your own question, haven't you?" Kyle said, in a strained tone that set off the tiniest bit of regret that I'd come down this road. "You're... not wrong about the 'type' I am. Or... have been. The wonderful guy, the baby, the house... I've lived that, and now... I don't anymore. I had the great love of my life, and lost it, and Morgan reminds me of him. So."

She picked up the bottle of bourbon, pouring herself another – generous – glass. In one gulp, she drank it down, with only a slight natural grimace in response to the heat the liquor generated in her chest.

"Should I assume that I *don't* remind you of the 'great love of your life?'"

Kyle scoffed, shaking her head. "No. Not at all."

"Because he – and Morgan – are wonderful, and I'm...?"

"A terrible person," she filled in for me, in a choked voice, but wearing a smile.

I raised my empty glass in her direction, motioning for her to pour. "I guess I'll drink to that."

She gave me enough for two shots.

And then gave herself more.

And then, we were eating and drinking and trading insults back and forth. We worked together, somehow, to clean up afterward, and I wasn't mad when we ended up together on the couch.

With the bottle.

"So uhh… how long are you staying around here?" I asked her after a long silence had passed between us.

"What's the matter?" she asked, smirking from the other end of the couch. "Afraid you'll miss me?"

"Nah. Getting too used to you, like how you get used to certain odors." I laughed when she kicked me – *when did she take off her shoes?* – and then grabbed her socked foot, pulling her toward me. What I *didn't* realize was that she still had that bottle of bourbon in her hand, and my sudden action made her spill it all over her sweater.

"*Shit,*" she muttered, struggling to her feet to frown at the stains. There was only a splash left in the bottle now, but she put it down on the table. "Sorry. I'll buy you another one."

"Not worried about that. But you should probably take that off. Get cleaned up. Come here. I'll help."

Her eyes were low from the bourbon – hell, mine were too – but she caught my meaning. She even played along with it enough to pull the liquor-soaked sweater off, tossing it aside. But then she didn't move. Her gaze was narrowed at me… *thinking.* Thinking about it too hard.

"What's the matter?" I asked. "You still need me to piss you off to get you in the mood?"

"No."

Whatever had made her hesitate, she got past it, sauntering up to stand between my legs. Immediately, I sat forward, and my hands went for the button and zipper on her shorts, making her laugh.

"I thought your angle was a drinking game, where we lick bourbon off of each other?" she asked, as I lowered her shorts and panties at the same time.

I bent a little more in my seated position to get them past her knees, then motioned for her to step out before I looked up to find her gazing at me, lip pulled between her teeth.

"Look," I started, planting my hands at the back of her thighs as I straightened. Her pussy was *right there* in my face, putting off heat, and an aroma of arousal that damn near had my mouth watering. "How about you let me lick whatever I want to lick? That's the game." I slid one of my hands down to her calf, using a grip there to pull her foot up to rest on the couch. With my eyes still on hers, I kissed the inside of her thigh, moving toward her center until I was close enough to taste her.

But I didn't.

I raised an eyebrow at her, waiting for her response.

"Yes. *Please*," she uttered, letting out a shuddering breath when I did, like she'd been holding it. I closed my mouth over her, inhaling deeply to breathe her in, letting the magic of her sex take over my senses.

I *knew* it would be like this.

A smarter man would've recognized that as a reason to not take this intimate step, but fuck it – I *had* to know.

And *goddamn* she hadn't disappointed.

Her soft, slick bare flesh was pleasingly sweet to my tongue, and her gratified utterances were like soul music to my ears. I grabbed her leg, shifting her so that her thigh was hooked over my shoulder and I could bury my face deeper in that glory. My hands gripped her ass, keeping her in place as her hand dug into my shoulder, clenching and flexing as I sucked her clit into my mouth. Already, her body was tensing with pleasure, and every nibble, every dip, every lap of my tongue only made her wetter, which only made me go harder.

I wanted it all.

And I tried my best to get it, burying my nose against her clit as I licked her. I used my fingers to spread her open, then covered her with my mouth, doing whatever I had to do to get her thighs shaking even more violently, make her dig her nails in further, to get her... *screaming.*

Yeah.

There it was.

I didn't back off until her knees were too weak for her to keep herself up, and I had to hook an arm around her waist to catch her and keep her from crashing to the floor.

Her eyes were still closed when I pulled her into my lap, but after a few seconds, they fluttered open. "*Why* would you do that to me?" she happily groaned, making me laugh.

"My bad. Been too long. I was starving."

For some reason that made her eyes narrow. "*Been too long?* You're telling me you're not community dick?"

"In *this* community?! *Hell* nah," I chuckled. "I mean, I don't get down like that period, but even if I did, it wouldn't be around here, where everybody knows everybody's business. And everybody tells my mother *my* business."

She laughed. "So what, you don't want anybody knowing you have sex? Everybody thinks you're a virgin – or under a celibacy vow?"

"I didn't say all that. I don't want the women around here gossiping about me."

"Oh please, men gossip *way* more about their conquests than women do."

I opened my mouth to refute that, then remembered...

"*See,*" Kyle giggled. "You can't even deny it. You told somebody about *me,* didn't you?"

"Maybe."

She rolled her eyes. "*Maybe,*" she repeated, in a deep tone that was supposed to mock my voice. "Who did you tell?"

"My cousins."

Her head tipped to the side, like she was thinking. "Those two corny ass firemen, from the storm clean up day?"

I chuckled. "Yeah, that's them."

"Good. I don't need them sniffing behind me, ugh."

"*Damn*, you don't have to do my family like that."

"I'm just *saying*," she shrugged.

I stared at her for a moment, absorbing that pretty ass face. "So... you're cool about that? About me telling them?"

"I told my sister, so... why wouldn't I be? Wait though... I told my sister out of pure information sharing – that's what we do. I'd bet good money that *you*, on the other hand... told your cousins about us to mark me as off-limits. Tell me I'm wrong."

Her eyebrows were up, and a smirk was on her face, practically daring me to defy her words. I wanted to – wanted to jab a sharp needle into the little bubble of her ego that was showing through.

"I can't," I admitted instead, opting to tell the damn truth. I couldn't articulate a reason now, just as I couldn't have then, weeks ago.

Nor did I need to.

Kyle didn't push the issue. Now that she finally had her bearings, she sat up, bringing her face to mine. "You smell like pussy," she told me. "Pussy and bourbon."

"It's a new mouthwash I'm trying out," I told her, just before my fingers touched the back of her head, digging into her hair as I pulled her closer, pressing my mouth to hers. She wasn't demure about it either, eagerly inviting my tongue between her lips to caress and taste and tease.

I dropped my hands to her back, easily undoing the clasp of her bra, and slipping the soft cotton down over her shoulders. Once I'd tossed it away, I sat back, letting her pull off my tee shirt, and then maneuver with my sweats and boxers.

Getting everything over the boot on my foot required a bit of finesse, but Kyle didn't complain. She moved to her knees in front of me, carefully peeling it over in order to avoid any harsh jolting, which was appreciated.

When she stayed on her knees to take me into her mouth... that was appreciated even more.

She was indeed a sight to behold, taking me down her throat like it was nothing, barely faltering when she gagged, creating a mess of saliva and pre-cum that felt... *fantastic*. She neglected nothing – hands and tongue and teeth and suction harmonized to perfection to suck me dry, leaving me with clenched fists and curled toes and a deep, *deep* confusion over why the hell her ex-husband had let a woman like this go.

But I wasn't about to think about it too hard.

My only concern was Kyle rising from her knees to straddle my lap again, stroking with her hands until my dick came back to life, so she could ride it. That seemed to be *her* only concern too.

Eyes closed, hands gripping my shoulders, knees locked against my sides as she rolled her hips into mine. My hands touched her breasts, cupping and squeezing, pinching the hard peaks between my fingers as she rocked harder, and faster, until we were *both* releasing again. She collapsed against me for the second time, her face buried in my neck as she tried to catch her breath.

"*Shit*," I muttered as she involuntarily clenched around my hyper-sensitive dick, still riding the wave of that repeat orgasm. I wrapped my arms around her, keeping her steady as my eyes closed – a natural result of the excellent food, sex, and liquor.

As Kyle's soft snores filled my ear, I realized the bourbon must've caught up with her too. It usually would've been nothing to pick her up, carrying her to bed with me, but with my injured ankle, that wasn't an option.

And besides that... I was honestly pretty damn comfortable.

So instead of waking her to move, I pulled the soft throw from its draped position on the couch, using it to cover both of us. I held my breath a little as Kyle shifted, mumbling something unintelligible before she snuggled impossibly closer, then settled right back into slumber.

Then I closed my eyes again and joined her.

"WHAT ARE YOU TWO UP TO?" I asked, my husband and daughter's smug faces giving them away. Their twin dimples were in full effect, and I narrowed my eyes as I looked around the kitchen, zeroing in on a small, wrapped package at my usual place at our dining table. "What's this?"

"Open it and see," Nova chirped, pushing her bright pink glasses up on her face. She was practically vibrating with excitement, which made me a little nervous – she'd gotten an experimental streak from her father that tended to manifest in... interesting ways.

"Open it," Jay urged, tag-teaming me. I lifted an eyebrow, searching his handsome face for clues, finding nothing but mischief in his eyes.

"Fine." I put my coffee mug down and picked up that little package instead. "Our birthday just passed, and Christmas is months away. What is this for?"

Nova's big brown eyes stretched wide. "Because I loooove you." She was getting more impatient, bouncing on the tips of the bright pink Nikes she'd worn every day since she unwrapped them on her 12th birthday. "Open it mama, before I have to go to school!"

Grinning, I tore into the simple wrapping to find... "A cell phone case?" I asked, turning it over in my hands. It didn't have any packaging, and it was a little... rough. Almost as if... "Nova, did you make this?!"

When I looked up, my baby girl and her father were both beaming with happiness.

"Daddy let me use the 3D printer in the science department, and showed me how to use it, but I did the design myself! You should've seen the first few, they were so bad," Nova gushed, launching into all the details she was dying to get out. While she was talking, I caught Jay's eyes, full of pride about his daughter. She was gifted – and not just in the way all parents thought their kids were, but truly a burgeoning future engineer, or whatever she found herself interested in next week.

Jay would nourish it, like he always did.

One of so, so many things I loved about him.

She was still going when Jay stepped out of the room and came back a few seconds later with my phone in his hands. He handed it to me, and I took off my store-bought case while they watched to put on the bright pink and purple one Nova had made.

It was a little crude, but it fit.

With it in my hands, I pulled her into a hug, then bent to plant a juicy, "ewwww-Mama!"-inducing kiss against her cheek. I took her face in my hands, looking her right in the eyes.

"I'm keeping this forever, my sweet SuperNova. I'll never take it off."

"BEN, WHAT THE HELL?" I muttered, pulling my head away from him. My eyes were still closed because I wasn't finished sleeping, but apparently he was done *letting* me sleep. I frowned harder as the unmistakably wet rasp of a tongue touched my face again. This time, I did open my eyes, intending to confront Ben about his apparent face-licking fetish.

It wasn't Ben's tongue.

When I opened my eyes, Domino was in my face, mouth hanging open, looking pleased with herself. My gaze traveled past the dog though, to the person standing behind her.

Regina.

Who, incidentally, looked quite pleased with herself too.

"Get up," she said quietly, in a tone that was nice enough, but didn't exactly invite any argument. "Help me take Dom on a little walk."

Beside me, Ben was sprawled out and snoring away, oblivious. Luckily for me, we'd woken up together on the couch hours ago, got in another round, and then showered before we climbed into his big bed.

I wasn't naked.

Thank God, I wasn't naked.

I'd been a little cold, so Ben had offered a tee shirt.

And then as a joke, I'd taken away the boxer-briefs he'd intended to put on and donned them myself. Instead of getting another pair, he'd slept naked.

He was naked.

Thank God, the blanket had him covered.

I looked at his sleeping form, wondering if I could scream loud enough to wake him up before Regina dragged me out to the woods to kill me, because what else could this "let's walk the dog" farce *mean*?!

"Come on, girl. Your shorts are in the living room," Regina called from somewhere near the front of the house.

"*Oh sweet Jesus,*" I whined, tempted to kick Ben to wake

him up. Instead, I dragged myself out of the bed and took my walk of shame to the living room to find my shorts and panties – neatly folded together on the couch, *fuck my life* – and then to Ben's laundry room. His fancy-pants washing machine dried as well, so my bourbon-soaked sweater that I'd tossed into it in the wee hours of the morning to mitigate potential stains was ready to go.

My socks were a lost cause.

Five minutes after she woke me up, I reported myself to Regina's presence at the front door, dressed and as presentable as a quick finger-comb, a splash of water on my face, and a rinse of mouthwash could get me.

"Come on," she urged, opening the door and stepping out.

She didn't have anything that could be used as a weapon... I didn't think.

"Well, this is... quite unexpected, right?" Regina asked, as Domino ran ahead of us on the trail behind Ben's house. "I suspected a little thread of... *something*, when it was you who got him out of the woods, but wow."

I pushed out a deep breath, trying to weigh my words before I spoke. "Regina... forgive me if I'm a little uncomfortable with this conversation. I don't mean *any* disrespect, but Ben and I–"

"Are none of my business," she confidently finished for me, even though *I* was going to say, *not something to get your hopes up about*. "I completely understand that. And I don't want you thinking this is something that I regularly do, because... well... frankly... I never have the chance. I come by here and let myself in to drop the dog off all the time, and I always step into the room to wake Ben and let him know. Only today... another vehicle was in the driveway. I thought maybe Luke, or one of my nephews had stopped by, but I didn't see anyone, and then I walk into the bedroom, and there you are."

I let out a nervous laugh. "Yes. There I was. In bed with

your son. Exactly what a mother wants to walk in on, right?"

Regina shook her head, not buying into my attempt at humor. "No, sweetheart, you don't understand – women are *never* here. Ben never brings women home. So this is... this is why I had to talk to you, because this is... exceptional!"

"Ms. Wilburn, I–"

"*Regina,*" she corrected me, waving me off. "I'm a modern woman myself, Kyle. I understand that spending the night with a man doesn't mean wedding bells are on the way – if it did, I'd be in trouble," she laughed. "Oh, I'm sorry honey. This is probably so awkward, but I ... I can't help feeling like this means something special."

"It doesn't," I shook my head. "Frankly, I'm not sure I can tolerate him beyond..."

I couldn't finish that sentence.

Not to his mother's face.

But apparently, I didn't need to, because she was laughing now, and shaking her head. "That's the same way I felt about that boy's father. *Jesus* that man got on my damned nerves. Did *that* until the day he died. But when he wasn't getting on my nerves – which was often. Very often. – he was absolutely the love of my life. And he gave me a son that was *just* like him."

My eyebrows lifted. "So... he's *always* been like that?"

"What, an asshole?" she laughed. "Oh yes, and he got it honest. But like his father did, he knows when to temper it and when to turn it up, always just the right level to where you don't know whether you're coming or going. Next thing you know, you're head over heels."

I scoffed. "Oh, I *don't* think I'm going to have that problem. I'm not here for that."

"What are you here for?" Regina asked, smiling. "You're finding yourself on the mountain?"

"Well... when you say it like *that*..."

"Oh no, I'm not teasing, honey. *Big Sugar* is a good place for that, real good! Just understand that while you're up here looking for yourself, you might find something else, too."

"Ms.... *Regina...* I'm not... in any position to find anything else. Certainly not what you're implying. And Ben would probably choke over what you're suggesting."

She waved that off. "Oh please, I know that boy left and right. No loose ends with that one. If he wasn't interested, trust me – you wouldn't be able to stand the sight of him – he'd have made sure of *that*."

"So you're telling me I've been seeing his *nice* side?"

"I'm telling you there's a *reason* he hasn't run you off. And it's not cause of what's between your legs."

Is she saying my pussy is trash?

"I should probably say that differently – I don't mean—"

"It's fine," I told her, shaking my head. "It's fine, *really*. I think we should probably head back though, and stop this incredibly strange conversation while we're ahead."

"Wait, please," she pleaded, grabbing my hands. "Let me... can I speak my heart for a moment, as a mother?"

I swallowed.

"I... yes, Regina. Of course."

She gave me a tight smile, then turned to look off in Domino's direction. "That's my grandbaby. The only one I can ever expect to have because I understand that my son can be... a complicated man. But he wasn't always."

I frowned. "But you said..."

"I know," she nodded. "But what we were talking about earlier, what he inherited from his father, is a personality thing. The man that he's become now... this is something different. We lost *Big* Ben when Benny was fourteen years old. Barely a teenager, and that... devastated him. He had his sharp tongue, sure, but he was generally a warm, well-liked kid. But then he wasn't. He kept everybody at arms' length, except his family, and the friends he'd already had before then. Anybody else? Never got a chance. I tried to talk to him, tried to get him to talk to his uncles and aunties, family friends, even a therapist, but... he wasn't interested. Never getting close to anybody was how he wanted to live."

I chewed at the inside of my lip as I listened to her speak about her son's pain, trying not to latch on to the familiar bits. I didn't *want* to relate to Ben, because that wasn't what this was about, not for me.

It was *not* why I was here.

"Then he met this kid, Devin. Oooh, bad-ass little monster, going around here setting fires and destroying whatever he could. He was headed for *real* trouble – sheriff was tired of hearing his mother begging for mercy, firefighters tired of running behind him. But Benny must have seen something in him. Sat him down with a stern voice, talked to him. Turns out... Devin was hurting too. Fourteen-year-old kid, who'd lost his father. Benny started mentoring him, got him a tutor, made him promise to stop giving his mother hell for finding a new husband, got him to accept and love his little sister... turned that boy's life around. Devin was even working with the volunteer firefighting program. And it helped Benny *so* much. I hadn't seen him so warm and social since his father passed – Devin was like a little brother to him." Regina stopped, shaking her head. "But then..."

"Devin Shaw?" I asked, swallowing the sudden tightness in my throat.

Regina nodded. "Yes. It was a big loss for the town. Ugly, *ugly* fire. You know that's how Benny got all scarred up?"

My mouth dropped. "I... no, I didn't.'

"He wasn't even on duty that night, but he... I... I've already said much more than I should. I'll let him tell you that story when he's ready, but... I only said all this for you to understand that my son isn't just an ass. He's grieving, Kyle. And I certainly don't mean to imply that it should excuse him, or that you should even accept it if he offends you, I just... he's an easy man to misunderstand. And I knew I'd seen a little change in him, but not why. Now I do."

I shook my head. "Regina, I'm not—"

"Falling in love. I know. *I know*. And I'm not saying he is either, but he's... feeling something." When her lips curved in a little smile, I realized there were tears in her eyes. "I'm just happy he's feeling *something*. Even if you're just having good sex and getting on each other's damn nerves – I'm *sorry*," she insisted, responding to my wide eyes and dropped jaw. "I'm not supposed to say that, but a mother wants certain things for her child, you know?"

I pressed my lips together and nodded. "Yes. I do."

Before I could speak again, Domino rushed up, licking my hand and running around me, excited about something.

"And Dom likes you. She doesn't like everybody." Regina said, as Domino took off toward the house.

When I turned to watch her, I noticed Ben standing at that back door that led to the kitchen. He was dressed now, and there was a spatula in his hand.

"Come eat," he demanded, of both of us. Then, he looked at me. "Don't believe anything my mother tells you."

Regina chuckled as she started back to the house, giving me a knowing look. She didn't speak, but I heard her loud and clear, even if I didn't want to.

Believe all of it.

Every word.

CHAPTER TEN

"Hello?!"
I dropped to a seat on my bed, using my shoulder to hold the phone against my ear while I pulled on my shoes. When there was no response, I spoke again.

"Hello? Mama are you there?"

"I *am*," she replied, finally. "Just overcoming my shock that you answered the phone."

"I *always* answer the phone," I corrected, in too much of a hurry to play along this morning. "Well, not always, but if I'm conscious and the phone is in my possession, I answer it when you call."

"You know what, you're right. You just never place any calls yourself. *That's* what it is."

"Mama..."

"I miss you," she continued as I got up, heading to the bathroom. I put the phone on speaker, then placed it on the counter while I wrestled my hair into a puff. "I haven't seen that gorgeous face in two months."

I opened my mouth for another correction, but doing the

math in my head... she was right. I *had* been in Sugar Valley for nearly two months now.

Doing nothing.

Except Ben...

"It has been a while, hasn't it?"

"Too long. It's time for you to come home. *Past* time."

"We talked about this, Mama," I groaned. "I'll be here until..."

"Until *what*? You still haven't explained to me what it is you're looking for."

I shook my head. "I'm not... I don't know how to explain. And I don't *have* to explain. I'm an adult, and this is where I want to be."

"You're being ridiculous. Once upon a time, you wouldn't have dared to be away from family, we were everything to you. You wouldn't even take Jay's last name, because you were a *Desmond*–"

"I didn't take Jay's last name because I was already establishing a career, with *my* name, when we got married..."

"We're the ones who've supported you through everything," she continued, like I hadn't spoken. "Graduations and medical school and weddings and pregnancies and funerals and—"

"*That's enough*," I snapped, putting down the brush I'd been using. "What you're doing – what you're trying to imply is *not* fair, and you know it isn't. I've clapped at every graduation, cried at every wedding, held hands at doctor's appointments, cheered at award ceremonies, and much more, my whole life. I love you. I love you *so much*, but you don't get to do this. You don't get to guilt me out of doing what *I* need to do to be okay. Not after what I lost."

"You think I don't want you to be okay?"

"I think... you want me in arm's reach. And I get it, Mama, I do. But my *needs* have to supersede your wants. I have to take care of myself right now, and being here... existing in a completely different way than I ever have before, is how I'm doing it."

She pushed out a harsh sigh. "That sounds so... *not* like coming to stay with me and your daddy and letting me fatten you up and watching my boyfriends Leon and Jethro with me."

I laughed. "I have binged NCIS with you way too many times to count. But I promise at least one more. I just need some time. Besides, it's only like an hour drive. You're acting like I'm across the world."

"You may as well be," she said, in a plaintive inflection that made my chest tighten. "We lost Jay, and our sweet Nova. We don't want to lose you too."

I closed my eyes, fighting back the threat of tears. "You haven't, Mama. Not ever, not if I can help it, okay?"

"Okay little girl," she answered, making me smile. "Jude said you met a man up there?"

"Jude needs to find some business," I countered, shaking my head. "Hey, I have an appointment that I need to get to, before I'm late. I love you. Always."

"I love you too. Be careful, you hear me?"

"I hear you, Mama. Bye."

I pushed out a sigh once we ended the call.

It wasn't exactly early in the morning, but it was too early to be emotionally exhausted when I hadn't even left my cabin yet. It was time to though, so I grabbed my things and headed out, making my way to Dr. Atwood's clinic.

I counted it as a win when I didn't see a truck parked outside, but opted against testing my luck. I parked and walked inside, waving to the receptionist before I headed back to Lilah's office.

"Hey there," Nurse Ellis greeted warmly as I walked in. "I

was just reassuring Lilah that you were coming. She doesn't want to be alone with Ben's fine ass."

"*Mean* ass," Lilah corrected, shaking her head. "Maybe since you'll be here as a buffer the appointment won't end with me plotting ways to kill him."

My eyebrows lifted. "I thought you wanted me here as a second opinion, to view his new xrays and all that since I was his... first responder."

"Oh yeah, that too," she gushed, with wide eyes. "But also... the other thing."

I looked between her and Justine, mind rolling, until I realized... "Lilah... do you have a crush on him?"

"What?! *Nooo*," she insisted, but then Justine cleared her throat and crossed her arms. "Okay... I used to. And I... may have asked him out. And he... may have laughed. And ever since then, I feel like it must be at the back of his mind whenever he sees me, because he's always so... detached."

Justine laughed. "Detached is that man's default state – I've explained that to you."

"Well, you're closer to his age, had classes with him. You know him better!"

"That had better not be your slick way of trying to sneak in an age jab," Justine started, and while those two engaged their good-natured back and forth, I was stuck on a question sparked by something Lilah said.

Why the hell would Ben laugh?

Lilah was attractive, smart, well-employed, sweet... *oh.*

That was probably the issue.

She was still in a tizzy over being in the room with him, based on something that didn't seem to be particularly recent history. Trying to go back and forth with that sharp tongue of his would eat her sweet, sensitive soul alive.

"So you're not saying that he was like... *cruel* to you, right?"

I asked, verbalizing a question that should have remained firmly in the confines of my mind, because it didn't matter – Ben wasn't a *dating* prospect for me.

Still, I'd be lying if I pretended her immediate denial wasn't relieving.

"No," she shook her head. "If that were the case, I'd refuse to see him, he could drive his ass to Blackwood or something."

Justine chuckled. "See what you're doing, Lilah? You're scaring her. *I* like Ben," she said. "No, he's not the friendliest, but when you understand that it's not personal, it's fairly benign. Unless it *is* personal. Then you might get your feelings hurt," she laughed.

"You might get your feelings hurt either way, tell the truth!" Lilah fussed. "Like I said, Justine was in school with him, from elementary or something. They're practically friends."

"Really?" I asked, and Justine shook her head.

"No. Lilah is used to men falling at her feet, so she has a complex about this one. All of this foolishness, and she doesn't even want him." Justine rolled her eyes as the phone rang, interrupting Lilah's response.

Lilah picked up the receiver, listening for a moment before she said, "Okay. Send him back." When she hung up, she looked right at me. "It should be a quick appointment, I promise. We're seeing if we can move him to the walking boot he has been hounding me about."

My eyes widened. "He's only been in the other one for what, two-and-a-half weeks?!"

She threw her hands up. "He insists on at least trying, and forwarded me a bunch of studies about how this particular boot got fracture patients mobile faster. I checked it out, and he's right. It all depends on his x-rays today though, and if the fracture is healing."

"Okay," I nodded. She was correct, but that didn't lower any

CHRISTINA C JONES

of the concern I felt. I didn't want him to end up worse off because he was trying to move too fast, but... we were supposed to take our patients seriously. If he wanted to investigate this, fine, we would.

But he would *not* be leaving in a walking boot unless I saw some improvement on that fracture.

Ben was already seated in the exam room when Lilah and I arrived, doing something on his phone, which I'd never even seen. She entered first, with her standard bubbly "good morning", receiving *his* standard grunted unintelligible reply, without looking up.

When *I* spoke, he took his eyes off that screen.

He didn't have to look as good as he did, not in a regular ass tee shirt and shorts, but he did. Maybe because I hadn't seen him in over a week, since that day I ended up eating pancakes beside his mother in second-day panties.

At least the pancakes had been good.

But the whole thing had been entirely too... *cozy*.

That whole conversation with Regina had uncovered some uncomfortable parallels between Ben and I that I had no interest exploring. I didn't want to bond, or relate. I just wanted to... *be*.

So.

I was staying away from him.

After this appointment.

He didn't even bother grunting at me, just lifted his head in the briefest possible acknowledgment before Lilah started running through questions about his ankle. Based on what he *said*, it did seem like he was healing, but ankle fractures were notoriously slow repairs. The x-rays would tell the *real* story.

Luckily for him... those stories matched up.

He undoubtedly had a ways to go, but Lilah and I were both confident putting him in a walking cast after he agreed to still take it easy for a few more weeks – especially after I took the extra steps on explaining the chances of him refracturing it, possibly requiring a surgery, or being off his feet *even longer* if he didn't take good care of himself now.

I helped Lilah with the actual fitting of the boot, and unless I was imagining it... Ben seemed excited. *Excited Ben* was an adorable-sounding anomaly I wanted no parts of, so while Lilah was giving him the last of her care instructions, I slipped out.

Not fast enough though.

More than once, Lilah had offered a detailed tour of the office, but I'd never taken her up on it. I wasn't in Sugar Valley to work – I was technically on sabbatical, but wasn't even sure yet that I'd ever set foot in Blackwood General again. Before, I hadn't wanted to be reminded of the hospital. But since that night in the forest with Ben, it had been eating at me.

The adrenaline rush of the emergency, the mental challenge of choosing the right course of action, the buoying realization of success, and perhaps most striking for me... the *aftercare*. It wasn't something I ever got to do anymore – participate in the quiet moments with the patient. For me, it was always the critical moments, the high stress, every-second-counts stuff.

Sitting and squeezing someone's hand in reassurance while they asked – and got answers to – all their questions?

Unheard of.

That was why curiosity led me to peek into an empty exam room to look around, marveling like a child at the way standards had changed since my last time in a non-emergency clinical setting. The brands were different, the magazines were an array of all shades of faces, even the simple paper exam gowns had changed – for the better.

"You avoiding me or something?"

Ben's voice nearly made me jump out of my skin.

I looked up to find him leaning in the doorway, smug as hell in his fresh new walking boot, but on his crutches still, as instructed. I slid the drawer I'd been looking through closed.

"Why would I do that?"

He smirked. "That's not answering the question."

"It isn't, is it?" I moved closer to where he was and leaned against the counter. "If I *was* avoiding you, how would you feel about that?"

He moved out of the doorway to be right in front of me, getting way closer than necessary. "Like you needed to get over it. I'm hungry."

"And what exactly does that have to do with me?" I asked, more intrigued than I needed to be by the potential double-meaning of his words.

"You have something I want to eat," he told me, resting one of his crutches against the counter to free his hands. I bit my lip to stifle my reaction as he hooked a finger in one of the front belt-loops of my jeans, pulling me toward him. "Or are you being stingy now? What are you cooking for us for dinner?"

"Us?"

"Yeah." He dipped his head in, raising an eyebrow at me. "You told me your secret, remember? So I know you've got extra."

Ugh.

He was right.

"Brown butter and honey-glazed salmon. Duck fat potatoes. Sauteed kale."

Ben nodded. "Yeah. *Hell yeah*, that sounds good. I'm gonna eat that. And then I'm gonna eat *you*. What time do I need to be there?"

"You have a lot of nerve. Are you *telling* me you're invited to dinner and dessert?"

He bit down on his lip, leaning in again until our mouths were almost touching. "You telling me I'm not?"

Before I could answer, we were joined by Justine, who... apparently hadn't noticed us there. She had on headphones, loud enough I heard the beat from whatever she had blasting in her ears, and a box of supplies in her hands, which she put down on the adjacent counter to free her hands.

To dance.

By the time her twerking turned her in our direction, her eyes were closed and her face was pulled into the kind of frown you wore when you were *really* into the music. Ben and I stood there, rapt, waiting for her to notice us.

When her eyes finally came open, she froze.

Her gaze bounced back and forth between Ben and me, mouth open. Then she clamped it shut, grabbed her box of supplies and left, like she hadn't seen anything.

"Oh *God*," I grumbled. "Isn't *this* wonderful?"

Ben sucked his teeth. "Man, I've known Justine a long time. She's cool. She won't say anything to Lilah." Something must've registered on my face, because Ben laughed. "Come on, I know she told you she tried to shoot her shot."

"Why would she tell me that?"

"Because that's what y'all do."

I frowned. "Who is *y'all*? You mean like how you told your cousins we slept together?"

"Man, why are you always bringing up the past?" he asked.

"Oh, *I'm* the one. I see."

Ben laughed. "Seriously though... what time?"

I wanted to say *no time*.

Never.

Let's stop here before we have a chance to get ahead... of ourselves.

"Six is fine."

That's what left my mouth instead.

Ben nodded, and then he was gone, and then I was letting

out a breath I hadn't even realized I was holding. And asking myself, for about the millionth time since I set foot in Sugar Valley... *Kyle, what the hell are you doing?*

Lilah was still in her meeting when I finally stepped out of the empty exam room after taking a moment to collect myself. I had every intention of sneaking out without saying anything to anyone, but before I crossed the threshold back into the waiting room, Justine swooped in, wrapping an arm around my shoulders.

"Oh no ma'am. *We need to talk.*"

She pulled me right back to that empty exam room, closing the door behind us.

"So that looked *cozy,*" she said, propping her hands on her hips. "Is it serious?"

"God, I hope not."

Shit.

I was going to have to see somebody about the truth coming out of my mouth when I didn't want it to.

Justine frowned. "Why? You look hot together!"

I sighed. "Maybe so, but I'm not in the market for serious. Hey, can you..."

"Not say anything to Lilah?" she scoffed. "Oh girl, you don't even have to ask. It would send her into an existential crisis, and I'm not trying to hear her mouth. Besides... you know what this meeting is about, right?"

I shook my head.

"She's looking to hire her replacement. She wants to move to the city – she *wanted* to offer this clinic to you, she didn't think you'd be into the small-town thing. Since *she's* over the small-town thing."

"Right," I nodded. "She's a great doctor though, so I'm sure she'll fare well."

"She definitely will."

"Sugar Valley is probably going to miss her though."

"We definitely will," Justine agreed. "But you know what would soften the blow?"

My eyebrows rose. "What?"

"If a certain bad-ass big-city surgeon who is done with that life took over her practice."

I drew my head back. "Meaning *me*?" I frowned. "Who said I was done with that life?"

"Everything about you says you're done with that life," Justine laughed. "If you weren't done with that life, you wouldn't be here. Or rather, you wouldn't have stayed *this* long. You're here to start over, and Sugar Valley is great for that. I'm trying to get my friend Eva here now."

"Why do you think it's great for starting over?"

She smiled. "It's quiet, it's beautiful, the people are friendly... well, except Ben, but you certainly haven't let *that* stop you."

"Oh *God*."

"I don't know why you're so embarrassed," she shrugged. "You could do worse around here. Like one of his corny ass cousins. Now *that* would be shameful."

We shared another laugh, but then she had to get back to work. I didn't have anything to do for the moment, so I took my time heading back to my lodge, settling in front of the TV.

I had a few hours before dinner.

"YES. YES. YES. YESSSSSS," I groaned, hooking my legs tighter around Ben's waist as he plunged into me with surprising, yet incredibly gratifying power. I was perched on the kitchen counter, and he was in front of me, with one knee bent in a chair we'd dragged up to make this work.

If he hurt that ankle again, he wasn't going to be blaming it on *me*.

"*Shit*," he grunted, driving in hard for one last stroke before he released. I'd already gotten mine – already gotten a couple, actually, since he'd made good on his intended eating. I clenched around him, making him curse again, this time in my ear.

God that feels better than it should.

"Hey, so... you're on some kind of birth control, right?" he asked as he pulled out. He couldn't immediately step away because of his propped leg, so apparently we were going to be face to face for this awkward conversation.

I lifted an eyebrow. "You don't think it's a little late to ask that, after we've had unprotected sex how many times now?"

"Better late than never?"

"Not... really... but luckily for both of us, pregnancy isn't even possible for me."

His eyes bucked, and I knew I should've just said, "Yes, I'm on birth control," and called it a night. I maneuvered myself down from the counter to head to the bathroom as he yelled after me.

"You're not going to elaborate on that?"

"Should I?" I asked, stopping and turning to face him. I was completely naked, which distracted him for a moment until he brought his eyes back to my face.

"We're having raw sex, so I'd kinda like to know if your pussy is like a black hole or something, yeah?"

My mouth dropped open. "Wow. *Wow*. That is such an incredibly awful thing to say, but... I guess that's kinda correct. I don't have a uterus... anymore. I had fibroids. Then I had a hysterectomy. And now I don't have fibroids."

He was silent for a moment, hands cupping his soft dick.

THE CULMINATION OF EVERYTHING

"Damn. So... you weren't messing around when you said it wasn't possible, huh?"

"Nope. And even if I *did* still have all the equipment, the chances of me *getting* a baby out of pregnancy were damn near zero anyway. So, yeah... no worries there."

Now that I'd led us down a sufficiently dark path of too much information, I made my way to the bathroom, where I immediately climbed into the shower, turning on the water as hot as I could stand. A few moments later, I heard Ben come in.

"So... 'damn near zero'... that means you've got a kid, right?"

I closed my eyes, wondering about the possibility of drowning myself with a showerhead. "I don't want to talk about that. I'm not about to talk about that."

"That's cool. I was just curious."

"Well, stop."

He didn't respond to that, but I heard him still in the bathroom – peeing, and then washing up. Eventually he left, and then I started feeling like the one who was an asshole.

It wasn't fair to drop crumbs and then get mad when he followed them.

When I got out of the shower, I dressed for lounging, in leggings and a comfy tee shirt. I found Ben dressed, in the kitchen, eating the extras from our meal straight from the pans.

"You weren't saving any of this, were you?" he asked, chewing.

I shook my head. "No, please. Enjoy."

He kept eating, and I joined him in the kitchen, leaning against the counter. For a few moments, neither of us said anything, but he did turn to look at me, like he knew there was something on my mind. Finally, I got tired of the staring contest.

"So... about earlier," I started, and he shook his head, immediately brushing me off.

"Nah, you're good. Everybody has their shit." He shrugged. "I'm pretty sure my mother gave you some of mine."

My lips curved up. "Maybe a little."

"Regina Wilburn doesn't tell *a little* of anything," Ben laughed. "Whatever she said, had you avoiding me."

"Right, it was *that*. Because your winning personality makes you such a pleasure to be around."

He shook his head. "You only want me when there's dick involved."

"And *you* only want me because there's pussy involved."

"That is *not* true," he insisted, looking offended. "You can cook too, so..."

A knock at the door interrupted me from responding, but I made time to flip him off before I moved to look through the peephole.

Shit.

I stepped away from the door and pulled my lip between my teeth, turning to look at Ben in the kitchen.

He smirked around a mouthful of potatoes. "It's Morgan's corny ass, isn't it?"

"Don't be like that."

"You're about to answer that door?"

"He can clearly see the lights on. I'm not going to be rude."

He sucked his teeth. "He showed up unannounced, that isn't rude."

"I'm going to see what he wants," I explained. "Give me a second."

Ben's expression was anything except pleasant, but I was sticking to my guns. Morgan and I hadn't even spoken in days – which I hoped meant he was taking the hint that I had avoided being alone with him since the *last* time he showed up here.

And kissed me.

I left Ben in the kitchen to open the front door, flipping the porch light on to step outside.

"Morgan, hey – how have you been?" I asked, accepting the hug he used to greet me.

"I've been good – that's actually why I'm here."

My eyebrows lifted. "Oh?"

"Yeah. There's a restaurant here that I stopped in, tried. Ended up talking to the owner, and he purchased several of my pieces to display in the lobby and dining room."

"Morgan, that's *amazing*," I gushed. "Congratulations! So... how does that work, do you have to go back home to get them, or?"

"A good friend is packing them up from my studio, and she's going to drive them up. There's going to be an event, all that."

I smiled. "Well, put me down on the invite list, I will absolutely be there."

Morgan started to say something but stopped, raising his head a little. "Did you hear something? What was that?" he asked. "Like a door slamming?"

"Uh... maybe one of the neighbors," I shrugged, even though I knew damn well it wasn't. I heard the distant sound of a vehicle starting, and knew that Ben had left through the back door of the lodge, using the stone-paved path to reach the rear lot where he'd parked.

"Yeah... well, anyway, I wanted to stop by and tell you the good news in person," Morgan said, smiling.

"Yeah, of course. Thank you. Congratulations again."

"Thank you, gorgeous."

He pulled me into another hug – this one lingered a little longer than it should, but he offered no resistance to me pulling away to pat his shoulder.

"Good night."

I didn't give the goodbyes a chance to linger like that hug.

I gave him a nod, and went back inside, closing and locking the door behind me. Sure enough, I was alone now. Even though I hadn't been particularly looking forward to Ben's company, something about his absence... stung.

Was he mad about me stepping out to talk to Morgan?

Surely that couldn't be... right?

Just a few weeks ago, he'd made it *explicitly* clear that he'd be glad when I left the mountain. A couple rounds of sex and a reset ankle couldn't possibly reverse that.

Not this fast.... *right?*

I shook my head.

It was a completely ridiculous line of thinking, something like this, with someone like Ben. He wasn't here looking for love any more than I was, and he'd left because he'd gotten what he came for.

A full belly and empty balls.

And I'd... gotten to orgasm, *twice*. I'd gotten to feed someone. I'd gotten to not be so goddamn lonely for those few hours.

We'd *both* gotten what we wanted.

So why did it suddenly feel so hollow?

CHAPTER ELEVEN

The memory was seared into my nostrils.

More than any of the fire safety my father had drilled into me from the time I was old enough to understand, more than my firefighter training to follow in his footsteps, more than the real experience of being part of the small team keeping Sugar Valley from succumbing to the occasional flames.

I remembered the night that smoke woke me up.

Or maybe it was Domino.

I never was sure, because it seemed like as soon as my eyes opened and my brain registered that something was wrong, she was frantic – barking and growling at the open window.

The sky over the trees was glowing.

It had been dry all year, to the point that we were jokingly calling it *Sugar Leaf Nawl* instead of Sugar Leaf Falls, because it was damn near to the point of drying up. All the visitors who came through the lodge got warnings, we put up special signs banning campfires, precisely so this *wouldn't* happen.

But there it was.

A wildfire.

My eyes had gone to my phone, wondering why no one had

called me. The best answer I ever got was that it was supposed to be my night off. *You'd been working fourteen-hour shifts for weeks, you needed a break.*

That had been my chief's decision. And it was *because* of that decision that I could barely stand to look him in his face.

He should've called.

There wouldn't have been much that my presence added to the fighting of the fire – by the time I got there, units from neighboring cities were on the way with air support, and our two trucks were fully manned, doing as much as they could to wet the forest around the blaze. Anything we could do to keep it from spreading.

It was chaos.

Because of the chaos, no one was paying attention to the house.

It was a small town.

We all knew the Shaws were in Blackwood, celebrating their anniversary. Their little girl was having a sleepover with her best friends, and so was their son.

It was supposed to be empty, but it wasn't.

I knew that.

Because *I* was the one who had responded to Devin's text, worried that his friends were about to get him into trouble with girls and weed – usual teenage shit, but *exactly* the kind of problem he didn't need. He was a volunteer with the fire department, and our chief did random drug tests.

Devin wasn't excluded from those, especially not when his ass had been a little troublemaker before. He was on his *last* strike.

He wanted to leave and go home.

I encouraged him to.

I thought I was saving him then.

I thought I was saving him when I burst into the house with no gear to bring him out. Unconscious.

Burning.

But alive.

They airlifted him to Blackwood, then stuck me into an ambulance, under duress. I hadn't even known I was injured until they were cutting the scraps of my clothing off me, asking questions I couldn't hear or answer, not with the oxygen mask they were forcing on me.

Trapping me with the smell of burned flesh.

We were never supposed to assume a building was empty – we were supposed to clear it, if we could. With the chaos of the fire, trying to keep it from spreading to more homes, up the mountain, etc... I knew why.

I just didn't accept it.

Never would.

"Are you even listening to me, dude?" Luke asked, and I shook my head without looking away from the burned section of the forest.

"Nope."

It was messed up, because I was only out here on his family's property to go over it with him, at his request. I had a clear view of the burned-out section of forest from here.

"Focus, bruh," he insisted. "What the hell am I supposed to do about this auction?"

I blinked. "What auction?"

"Are you *serious* right now?" he asked, shaking his head. "I told you the whole story – some type of tax shit, or something. I'm still trying to figure it out, but the land and all that... it's only still ours until after this property auction. The starting bid is going to be forty-thousand dollars that I don't have."

"Shit... they won't work something out? A payment plan for what's owed or something?"

Luke adjusted the fedora I'd already roasted him about on his head. "Nah. It's too far gone. Maybe if I'd come back earlier, but I didn't know. They never said shit to me about it. I could've helped before it got to... *this*.

He waved his hand, gesturing at the property that surrounded us. *Honeybranch Vineyard and Winery* was defunct now, but Luke and I had spent plenty of time playing hide and seek amongst the colossal wine barrels as smaller kids, and then sneaking up here with girls as high schoolers, getting drunk off the bottling remnants. His grandmother's sickness had been the catalyst for the steady decline, and then her death brought it all to a grinding halt.

That was more than five years ago, and had been the thing that drove Luke away from Sugar Valley. Now, his grandfather's impending death had brought him back.

"They're talking to me about hospice care, man. Talking about keeping him comfortable for the next few weeks. Not even a year. Not months. *Weeks*."

I shook my head. "I'm sorry, man. That's rough."

"Yeah. Not much I can do though, other than making sure things are smooth. I guess I'm packing up the house, getting all our stuff out before it's bought by some... I don't know. What kind of person buys a defunct winery on a mountain?"

"Beats the hell out of me," I shrugged. "Maybe nobody will buy it. The auction just passes, nothing happens?"

"I'm not sure. But... hell, maybe it'll give me some leverage to get it back. Get it up and running again."

I nodded. "Yeah. Live out your grandparent's memory."

Luke turned to me, frowning. "Listen to you, sounding all sentimental and shit. Messing around with that doctor chick got you going soft?"

"Not at all," I chuckled. "Just saying... I lost my Pops, remember? So I know what it's like to... want to do something that honors them. You and your granddad never got along, but Mrs. Georgia was your world. Grandma's boy," I teased him, and he shook his head. "You want to bring this all back to honor her. I think it's a good idea. That's all."

"Yeah well... we'll see. Granddad's selfish ass probably let it go on purpose."

"You really think he'd do that shit?"

Luke scoffed. "Hell yeah, I do. He never liked me – just tolerated me being there. And once she was gone, he didn't have a reason to tolerate me. She wanted this place to go to me, which is why he stopped paying the taxes."

"It was probably medical bills dude, not spite."

"You don't know him like I do," Luke countered. "Either way... what's done is done now. I just have to deal with it going forward."

"All you can do, bruh. If you need some help packing or something, I've got you."

"Appreciate it man," he told me, bumping fists with mine. "I still think ol' girl has you going soft though."

I grunted. "It's not even like that. We're messing around, but that's it. She's gonna leave and go back to the city, find a lawyer, or an orthodontist or something, settle into a cushy life. She ain't thinking about Sugar Valley."

"But... you want her to?"

"Now you're putting words in my mouth," I countered. "We're having a good time."

"That's the thing – it's not just a good time with you, bruh. Didn't you say she spent the night at your house?"

"That doesn't mean shit."

"You don't even believe that yourself, do you?" Luke laughed.

"I gotta get outta here man," I told him, actively ending *that* line of conversation. "I'm back on a few of my ranger duties, and

CHRISTINA C JONES

I need to prove I can get the shit done so they can send my replacement back to the other side of the mountain where his ass belongs."

"Right. I'm sure not wanting to talk about Kyle Desmond doesn't have anything to do with the timing."

"Oh, it has *everything* to do with it," I admitted, chuckling. I called for Domino, and Luke and I parted ways so I could go about my business.

But now he had Kyle on my mind.

I'd been trying *so* hard not to think about that shit, because every time I did it made me inexplicably mad. I had no claim to her, and wasn't trying to.

So then why did her answering the door for Morgan piss you off?

I didn't know.

Couldn't explain the shit, not even to myself. It was easy to rationalize – the sex was good, the food was good, and her face wasn't bad either.

But it felt like more than that, somehow.

It wasn't as if we'd had some deep enlightening conversation, like we enjoyed having the other around – we were tolerating each other. None of the things that came to mind when you thought about "falling for someone".

Falling for someone wasn't even... a thing that I did.

It wasn't in my make-up, or my vocabulary.

So I didn't know what this shit was.

This shit being the annoying ass pull I felt to be around this woman who was nothing like me, at all. We didn't like the same things, think the same way, have the same life experiences... we had nothing in common, at all.

So why the *fuck* was I feeling this weird attachment to her?

It pissed me off, adding fuel to the ire I'd woken up with, and been carrying around all day. I didn't know how to sift through so I didn't even try – I focused on completing my tasks in the forest with Domino at my side, then took my ass back home where I showered and all that.

Then, I went to my refrigerator.

The first thing I saw was Kyle's bowl.

Shit.

I closed the refrigerator, filing a need to clean it out in the back of my mind for later. Instead of trying to fix something for myself, I threw on some clothes and got in the truck, heading up to the lodge to eat at *Maple*.

And drink at *Maple*.

I slipped in and headed straight to my usual spot at the bar, tucked into the corner. Despite my carefully built surly reputation, there was always *somebody* that wanted to talk anyway, and this wasn't the night for that.

Not at all.

Luckily, nobody seemed interested in bothering me.

I was considering that a small blessing until a familiar laugh met my ears. I looked up from my bourbon to take in my surroundings for the first time, and that's when I spotted her.

With *him*.

It wasn't just them – it was a group, but still. She was seated beside him, laughing at his corny ass jokes – I didn't need to hear it to know – and not backing away from it when he touched her. Shaking my head, I turned my attention back to my nearly empty bourbon, then waved the bartender over.

I was going to need another drink.

And some damn food, since my hunger was only adding fuel to the low-level rage I'd been feeling all day.

After dinner and another drink, the sound of that group was still grating on my nerves. Instead of hanging around to be pissed off, I closed out my tab and then headed to the bathroom to relieve myself before I took my - admittedly –

grouchy ass home before I took it out on anybody except my bed.

I was a little tipsier than I thought, and moving slow on my crutches to make up for it. Driving probably wasn't the best idea, so I resolved to move to a table tucked away from Kyle and her loud ass group, somewhere with a TV, while I waited for the liquor to wear off.

Well... that was the intention.

What *happened* was that on my way out, Kyle was coming up the hallway toward the bathroom too.

"Oh, hey!" she greeted, offering a smile that made me even *more* pissed off.

I didn't want to be an asshole to her though – a first – so I grunted a passable response and kept walking, but I guess that wasn't good enough.

"Back on *that* today, are we?" she asked, and I stopped walking to turn around.

"Never should've gotten off it, to be honest."

She frowned. "Um... okay. If that's what you want, fine, but... are you mad at me or something?"

"No," I countered. "Not bothered at all. Why would I be?"

"I have no idea, but... you *seem* bothered. That's why I asked."

"And I told you I wasn't, so... have fun with your little boyfriend."

I'd messed up.

As *soon* as I said that shit, I wished I could snatch it back into my mouth, but obviously that wasn't happening.

Kyle smirked. "*Oh.* That's what this is about? You're jealous of Morgan?"

"Jealous?! Why the hell would I be jealous of him?!"

"I don't know."

"Damn right you don't know," I replied, shaking my head. "What would I look like, being mad about that corny ass dude? We had our fun, right? I can fall back, you and him live it up. Have fun. Maybe. He's your type, right? I see exactly what your type is. And you said he reminded you of your ex-husband, right?"

"Ben, don't do this," Kyle asked, raising her hands. "This isn't a topic that—"

"*Oh*, is that off-limits too? Don't talk about your kid, don't talk about your corny ass husband?"

"*Ben.*"

This time, the shit sounded like a warning, but the bourbon had my tongue too loose to heed it.

"What happened, huh? I didn't think corny men screwed up bad enough for their women to drop them, so this is interesting to me. What was it, he wouldn't get a job? Drank too much? Fucked your bestie? Went to work and never came home? – *Shit!*"

I didn't see her hand coming until it was too late to avoid it – she'd already smacked the hell outta me.

"You don't know *shit* about me," she said through gritted teeth, emotion choking her voice and filling her eyes with a gloss of tears. "*Fuck you!*"

She turned to walk away, brushing past my mother who walked up with concern etched on her face. "What was that about?! Did that heifer *hit you*?"

"It's fine, Mama," I insisted, not wanting her to get started, but the truth was that it stung like a bitch. "I said some shit about her ex-husband."

My mother's eyes went big. "*Ex*-husband?"

"Yeah, she was married before."

"I know *that*," she hissed. "But he's not... what did you say to her?"

I shrugged. "I don't even remember, I don't know! I'm tipsy, shit. Something about him not coming home."

"Oh *no*," Mama groaned, clutching hands to her chest. "Oh, Benny, *no*!"

"What are you moaning and groaning about, woman? She shouldn't be so sensitive about the shit, she's not the first woman to get a divorce."

"She's not *divorced*, Benny!"

My eyes narrowed. "What are you talking about? You're saying she's *still* married?"

"No. I... a few weeks ago, when I saw her at your house... I said something to her about being a mother. She didn't say anything, but she had this look in her eyes that made me feel like something was off. So I looked her up, *again*, looking for stuff from her personal life. I couldn't have her sniffing behind my son if she was actually some type of criminal or something, right?"

"Is she?"

"*No*. That's not what I found."

"But you found *something* and didn't tell me... why?"

"Because I didn't want to meddle, because if I meddled, you wouldn't be interested in her anymore," she answered, in a tone that clearly implied she thought that should've been obvious. "I was leaving you alone to your business."

"Oh *now* you decide to. Turning over a new leaf, are we?"

"You're about to get smacked a second time," she warned. "Now I want you to go apologize to her!"

I scoffed. "For *what*? Obviously ol' boy was trash, or they would still be together. But hell, you just said she wasn't even divorced, so I don't know what to think now. Are you going to tell me what you found?"

"No," my mother said, shaking her head as she pulled out

her cell phone. "You need to see this for yourself."

IT STARTED RAINING, but I was too mad to care.

I stomped from *Maple* all the way back to my cabin in a downpour, peeled myself out of my soaked clothes, used the bathroom, then got in the shower.

Where I cried my eyes out.

He went to work and never came home?

Yes.

He did.

The goodness of that morning... *haunted* me. Exactly two weeks before that morning, we'd fought. One of the worst of our marriage, but nothing outside of the usual stuff busy, married parents fought about. The bathroom not being clean enough, the in-laws, not spending enough time together, not enough sex,

The usual suspects, just all together, compounded by the fact that we'd been too damn busy to have the small fights, so we had that big one.

I asked him if we were going to work. If we were staying together, because in that moment of rage and hurt and frustration and exhaustion, it felt impossible.

He looked me in my face, and told me, *"You're goddamn right we are."*

Which was relieving, because I couldn't live without him.

I thought I couldn't live without him.

Hell, I still wasn't sure.

But that morning, two weeks later, was perfection. The kind of love-filled morning that made you wonder if it was what heaven was like.

Later, I wondered if Jay knew that would be our last morning, if that was why he'd turned the dial all the way up to *max* when we'd made love. If Nova knew – if that's why she'd given me that gift from her heart, with none of the pre-teen angst or attitude.

They couldn't have, but I wondered.

It was my day off that day.

I started to ask them both to play hookie with me, to stay home and binge movies and eat ourselves sick with sweets. But Jay had a test to give, and Nova had one to take, so I swallowed my selfish request and sent them on their way with kisses and climbed back into the bed, alone.

Hours later, a call from the hospital director woke me up. She was so sorry, but she needed me to come in and help.

"*A horrific accident at the school up the street,*" was what she called it.

It wasn't a fucking "accident".

A man walked into a middle school lunchroom and opened fire, taking out his anger against his estranged wife on purpose. He smiled his way past the decorative security guard on purpose, lied about his kid – a name he stole from his wife's old classroom rosters - leaving his backpack at home on purpose. He bought bullets, and Kevlar, and weapons explicitly built to maim in the worst possible ways, *on fucking purpose.*

Death was the purpose.

Terror was the purpose.

But they never wanted to call it what it was unless there was brown skin involved.

Faintly, I registered that someone was knocking on my door.

I didn't want to answer, so I wasn't *going* to answer, but whoever it was wouldn't go away. I climbed out of the shower, wrapping myself in a robe to stomp to the door, fully prepared to curse Morgan's ass out – he was the only one who hadn't taken the hint to leave me alone when I returned to the table earlier for my purse.

It wasn't Morgan at the door.

It was Ben.

Soaking wet, and still tipsy if the half-open state of his eyelids was any indication. He was hanging in my doorway wearing an expression that suggested he was prepared to wait there all night, if necessary, and I was halfway tempted to make him.

"I'm sorry," he said, meeting my gaze. "I didn't know." When I didn't say anything, he repeated himself. "I didn't know."

I tightened the belt of my robe and nodded. "Okay."

"*I'm sorry.*"

"Okay."

I started to close the door, but he easily blocked it. Because I didn't have the fortitude to argue about it, or go back and forth, I didn't. If he wanted to be in the cabin, fine.

I'd be by myself, in the bathroom.

"*Kyle!*" he called after me when I turned to walk away. I heard the door close, heard his awkward footsteps, but didn't turn around until I heard him curse – just in time to see him fall flat on his ass.

"*Sh*it, are you okay?" I asked, rushing to where he'd landed. "Did your ankle take any of the fall?!"

He huffed, then laughed. "Nah, my ankle was in the air. Apparently, wet crutches don't play well with polished hardwood floors."

"Where are you in pain?"

"My ass," he answered. "And yours. I'm *sorry*."

I shook my head. "Ben, you don't have to—"

"Nah, I do." I was standing over him, but he grabbed my hand. "I *do*. All the other shit aside, I *never* would've said that shit to you if I'd known what happened to your family. I just... I've mentioned your ex before, and you didn't correct it, and when I brought up you having a kid—"

"Would *you* want to talk about it?" I asked. "Do you want to talk about Devin?"

He grunted. "*Hell no.*"

"Well, there you have it."

"I'm *sorry*."

"You keep saying that."

"I didn't know."

"You keep saying *that* too, like it matters!" I shouted, snatching my hand away from his. "Even if Jay and Nova were still alive, even if he was my 'ex' husband, why the hell would you say something like that to me?! What the hell have I done to deserve a jab like that, huh? Why would you *purposely* try to hurt me?!"

"Because, I... I don't know!"

"Don't know, or won't say?" I countered. "Because I find it hard to believe that you said that shit just because."

He shook his head. "It wasn't. I ... *fuck*. I don't know how to... articulate it. Not when I don't even fucking understand it."

"Oh God, just answer the question! Don't articulate, just... *say it*."

"I don't want that motherfucker in your face, okay?!" he growled. "And yet, his ass is always in it. It seems like you like that, and it pisses me off, because I don't fucking want you to."

I sucked my teeth. "Why do you even *care*?!"

"Because... goddamnit, because *I* want you!"

I blinked.

Then blinked again.

And again.

Because... *what?*

"Ben..." I started, shaking my head. "I... don't... I don't even know how to feel about that. What to do with it. How to accept it. I don't... I don't know how to be wanted like that, right now. How to want you back."

He shrugged. "Shit, neither do I."

"So what are we doing? What are you asking? What do you want from me?"

"All these damn questions," he grumbled, pulling himself up to his knees. I was about to offer him help to get up, which is what I thought he was doing.

Instead, his hands reached for the belt of my robe.

"What the hell are you doing?" I asked, trying to pull it back together as he pulled it apart. "I *know* you don't think I'm —*ahhhh, shit.*"

Whatever I was going to say got lost as soon as his mouth covered my pussy. My knees buckled as his tongue slipped between my folds, and I dropped my hands, bracing them against his shoulders.

"Ben—"

"*Shhhh.*"

I should've been mad about him "shushing" me, but it was incredibly hard when he'd done it right up against my sensitive skin, creating a delicious rush of air that made me all... *tingly.*

"*No,*" I whimpered, pushing his head back. "You said something really damn hurtful to me."

One of his hands grabbed my ass, nudging *me* forward since I'd pushed him away. The other slid between my thighs, slipping two fingers into me and pressing his thumb against my clit. "I'm trying to apologize, right now."

"Sex isn't an apology."

"You sure?" he asked, meeting my gaze as he stroked me with his fingers.

I shook my head. "What the hell are we doing?"

Ben's fingers stopped moving, but he held our gaze for a moment before he spoke. "Learning."

"What?"

"You said you didn't know how to do... this. To do... *us*. I don't either. So I guess we have to learn."

My eyebrows lifted. "*Have* to? As opposed to...?"

"As opposed to nothing. I don't see a different option."

And then he returned to what he was doing.

My mind was reeling, trying to process the moment, but it was impossible with his mouth on me. So I stopped. I pushed everything else from my mind and gave myself over to being pulled down to the rug and... apologized to.

Over, and over, and over.

Maybe he couldn't verbalize the necessary words, so he articulated with hands and tongue, and dick for good measure.

To highlight his sincerity, or something.

I told him his apology was accepted when I came the last time.

Afterward, when he was snoring in bed, I tried to figure out how the hell my night had ended... like this. I'd stormed out of *Maple* hot as fish grease, wishing I'd left him and his broken ankle right where I'd found him that night in the forest.

And now... he was taking up more than his fair share of space in my bed.

"You said you accepted my apology."

The sound of his voice in the darkened room made me jump. I hadn't realized his quiet snores had stopped, but apparently he'd been awake long enough to know I was up too, thinking in the dark.

"Nothing said during sex counts."

I felt him shift toward me. "So you changed your mind. You don't forgive me now?"

"I don't know."

"You should."

I couldn't see him, but I looked in his direction. "Why? Because you didn't know that my history made it a *completely* horrible thing to say, instead of just regular horrible?"

"Because I'm an idiot."

I raised my eyebrows, but didn't say anything. I waited for him to explain.

"I... saw your pictures. Your birthday album. I should've known it wasn't the type of thing you would've brought with you on a trip after a divorce. I should've... realized that you were grieving. Not... what I thought you were."

"Which was what?"

"Stupid. Sorry."

I let out a soft laugh. "That's not even remotely surprising. You always thought I was stupid."

"But in hindsight... I should've recognized what I was so familiar with myself. I'm judging you for going out in the storm over a phone that probably has important pictures, or maybe it was your husband's, or a gift, or... whatever. What you did to get it back was less dangerous than running into a burning house."

I swallowed. "The phone isn't the important part. The case is. My little girl made it for me. And gave it to me, the day that they... didn't come home. And, running into a building to save a life isn't the same as risking your life to save an object. No matter how sentimental it is. It was stupid."

"It wasn't stupid. It was... grief. It's a complex thing."

"Yeah," I nodded, blinking back tears. "It is."

There was silence between us for a moment before he spoke again.

"You saved lives that day. A lot. Even though the article said you'd gotten the news about your husband and daughter."

"Yeah."

I knew precisely which article he was talking about – that article was the only reason I knew many of the details about that day, because I had no real memory of anything after the phone call asking me to come help with the massive influx of critical patients.

It was a blur to me.

I was saving the ones other people loved because I couldn't save my own.

"Your husband... he covered kids with his body. Covered your little girl."

I closed my eyes, wiping tears from my cheeks. "Yeah."

"He was a good man."

"So are you."

"I didn't save anybody."

"But you tried."

"Nah. I failed."

"You gave his mother a few hours of hope. You did your best. That's not a failure."

There was silence, and then, "It still feels like one. Every day."

"I understand."

"I'm sorry."

I opened my eyes. "For what?"

"For saying what I said about Jay. For trying to hurt you. For being an asshole."

The corners of my lips turned up. "Okay. Apology accepted. Don't stop being an asshole though."

"Don't worry. I didn't plan on it."

CHAPTER TWELVE

I woke up in bed alone.

That wasn't what pulled me awake though – someone had knocked on the door.

I waited, staring at the empty place where Ben had spent the night, wondering when he'd left, since his residual warmth was still lingering in the sheets.

Then the knock sounded again.

I rolled over to see the digital clock, frowning when I realized it was almost ten in the morning – later than I usually slept. Pulling myself from the bed, I stretched, shaking the sleep from my limbs before I grabbed my robe, putting it on as I headed for the front of the cabin.

As soon as I stepped around the corner to the living area, I froze.

Ben was at my door, on crutches, wearing nothing but his boxers and his boot.

My parents were on the other side of the threshold.

Jude and my brother-in-law and nephew were behind them.

"Your family is here," Ben turned in my direction to announce, gesturing toward them, seemingly oblivious to the collective discomfort of whatever the hell was happening right now. Everybody was looking at me – I could only imagine what they were thinking, Ben nearly naked, me in my robe and bonnet.

Him having *obviously* spent the night.

The next thing I knew, Ben was ambling toward me on his crutches, stopping beside me to lean in and plant a soft kiss against my lips. "I've gotta get out of here. I was supposed to be up on the mountain an hour ago. I'll see you later."

"Um... oka—*ah!*" I let out a yelp as Ben smacked my ass in my short robe, then kept on past me to the bedroom. My gaze followed him in disbelief until he disappeared around the corner.

Only then did I turn back to my unannounced, uninvited family.

My father held up a cardboard tray of coffee, and my mother held up a large paper sack.

"We brought breakfast!"

My lips parted. "How... wonderful." I forced a smile to my face as they stepped inside, all smiles. "Here you all are. Without calling first. No warning or anything," I said, looking directly at Jude, who was unusually interested in the architecture of the lodge.

"Well, we didn't get to celebrate your birthday with you," My father explained, bending to press a kiss to my cheek before he moved toward the kitchen area with the coffee. "So your mother thought this might be a nice surprise."

"Surprise!" my mother gushed, pulling me into a one-armed hug. She followed my father to the kitchen while I greeted my brother-in-law and nephew, then turned my sights on Jude, who already *knew*–

"They ambushed me this morning," she hissed into my ear

as we embraced. "I tried to call you, *and* I texted a few times on the way up. And now I know why you haven't answered."

"You couldn't talk her out of this?"

Jude let out a shout of laughter. "Oh girl, you're funny. Have *you* ever talked Cookie Desmond out of anything?" After a moment of silence, she nodded. "Yeah. That's what I thought. Now..." she grabbed my hands, looking me right in the face. "Now, if you're still wearing that robe when we sit down to eat this food, I will *not* be able to stop your mother from asking about that man in front of Daddy."

"Good call," I agreed. "I'll be right back."

I found Ben seated on my bed, eyes closed, pain etched into his face as he stretched his arm out. I'd already not been confident that last night's fall had left him injury-free, and this made it worse.

"You want me to look at it for you?" I asked, closing the door behind me as I stepped into the room to put some clothes on.

He looked up and scoffed. "So you can put me in another torture device? Thanks but no thanks." He picked up his shirt, which looked *exactly* like it had been taken off wet and tossed on the floor to dry into a mess of wrinkles. "Your family seems nice. And your mother is *fine*."

"Okay what the hell is this?" I asked, shaking my head as I pulled out leggings, a tee shirt, and a flannel, which had quickly become my Sugar Valley "uniform". "What the hell are you doing?"

His eyebrows lifted as he pulled the shirt on. "I didn't realize I was doing anything."

"You're acting like... like you're my boyfriend or something," I blurted, fully realizing how ridiculous it sounded to be complaining about such a thing, but... that's where we were. Where *he* had taken us.

"I'm not anybody's *boyfriend*, Kyle." He stood, facing me

full-on. "I'm a grown ass man. And besides that... how do you want me to act?"

"*Natural.*"

He laughed. "This *is* natural."

"Answering the door for my parents in your boxers, is *natural?* Smacking me on the ass in front of my father is *natu*—I see your point. I do," I admitted as he smirked at me.

"In my defense, I didn't know it was your people. There's some rain or something on the peephole, so I couldn't actually see them until the door was open."

I squinted. "*How* is that a defense? You shouldn't have answered my door for *anybody* in your boxers."

"I was hoping it was Morgan," he shrugged. "So I could put *that* situation all the way in the ground."

"There is no situation to put in the ground," I half-laughed, half-growled. "You have been on him since that wilderness class, and I don't understand why!"

"You don't understand why I might want to punch a motherfucker who bursts out singing in the middle of my class in the throat? *Who does that shit?*"

"Morgan does, obviously," I countered.

And Jay would've too.

Which is probably why Ben was so... impossibly appealing.

I'd already been blessed to experience one great love of my life, with a man who was sweet, and funny, and lowkey, and would rather eat his own tongue than purposely hurt my feelings.

And then there was Ben, who was so *completely* different.

Such a jerk, but—

"Hey." When I looked up, he was right in front of me. I barely had a chance to react before he was burying his hands in the hair at my nape, pulling me into a kiss. "I'll see you later. I gotta walk back up to the restaurant for my truck."

I bit back a smile.

A jerk, but not only that. Maybe more.

"Okay. Um... I'll walk you out."

When we stepped back into the main area, my family had already arranged themselves around the table.

"Alright y'all!" Ben called out, stopping to toss his hand up for a wave before he went back to maneuvering with his crutches.

"Keep moving," I hissed as my family returned his greeting, knowing the chances of him getting stopped to talk were dangerously high between my mother and father.

At the front door, he turned to me. "Hey... before I go, I want to tell you something that's been on my mind," he said, seriously.

Frowning, I stepped out. "What is it?"

"So... you're cute and all that, but... brush your teeth before you sit down with your family. Your breath is on *ten*."

"If you don't get your ass out of here!" I shrieked, shoving him with my foot as he moved faster than I thought he could on those crutches. He caught himself from falling, then turned to wink at me.

I rolled my eyes, turning to go back inside. But I couldn't help glancing back, and he was still standing there with that annoying ass smirk, like he already knew I wouldn't be able to resist.

"Bye Kyle."

"Goodbye, Ben."

"Sooo... are we still pretending that fine ass hunk of chocolate didn't answer Kyle's door?"

Jude blurted that out as soon as my father, brother-in-law,

and nephew parted ways from us, intending to hike in the mountains while I showed Jude and my mother around town. To their credit, or something, no one had asked about Ben while we ate breakfast – it was my personal, grown-ass business.

But it was eating at them.

And now, apparently, my time was up.

"Yes," I answered, at the same time that my mother said, "*Hell no.*"

I groaned as they both stopped walking the path down to Main Street to round on me, hands propped on their hips.

"Kyle Yvette Desmond, you *will* tell me who in the world that man was at your door," my mother demanded, and Jude's ass chimed in with "*Yeah!*" like she didn't already know.

"They should've named you Judas," I told my sister, then turned to my mother. "*That man* is one who I can't decide if I'm mad at or not, and definitely shouldn't have answered my door."

"Mad?" Jude stepped forward, fists clenched, ready to fight if necessary. "What did he do to you?!"

"Obviously it wasn't *too* bad if the sex was enough to make her uncertain," my mother mused, head tipped, her gaze thoughtful.

I groaned. "The sex isn't what has me uncertain. It's... *everything.*"

"You still haven't said what his ass did," Jude pressed. "He's down to three working limbs, I could probably take him."

"I don't need you to fight anyone," I laughed. "It's just... he made a pretty horrible comment about Jay not coming home." Immediately, my mother and sister's expression turned murderous, but I held up my hands. "In fairness, he didn't know the details. Just that I'd been married before, not that he'd passed away. He thought I was divorced."

"It was still a fucked-up thing to say – sorry mom," Jude

said. "*Why* was he answering the door in his boxers if he did *that*?!"

I sighed, looking down the tree-lined road toward the town. "Because he... apologized. And he explained. And I accepted his sincere apology because I... don't want to be angry. I didn't come here for that. If I hadn't answered the door, he would've deserved it. If I hadn't accepted his apology, had just sent him packing, he would've deserved that too. But... *why*? To spend my night alone, crying over what he said?"

"Accepted apologies and orgasms *do* sound like a better way to spend the night," Jude admitted. "But *still*."

Laughing, I nodded. "Yes. Exactly. *But still*. I... feel guilty for *not* being mad, like it's an insult to Jay's memory. That wasn't how Ben intended it. He was drunk, and jealous, and lashing out, which *isn't* okay. But in context... he's not a man who forms emotional attachments easily. For him, it probably looked like I was choosing someone else, and it hurt, so... he wanted to hurt me. He didn't understand that his words weren't the paper cut he intended. They were more like a knife to the heart."

"Sometimes the people we care about mess up. They say the wrong things. You were with Jay almost half your life – I'm sure he's said some things that caused a sting," my mother replied. "The man is human. You can give him this one pass."

My eyebrows lifted. "Are you seriously Team Ben, after he answered the door in his boxers?"

"We're Team *Kyle*," my sister intersected. "You came here to... thaw. And baby that is one *hot* piece of man."

"The right temperature for the job," my mother giggled, and I covered my face with my hands.

"*What in the world is happening right now?*" I muttered into my palms as they laughed at me.

Jude pulled my hands down, tugging me to get me to start

walking again. "All jokes aside sis, as long as you're good, I'm good. Life is too short to be angry with somebody for the hell of it, if that's not even what you feel."

"But I don't *know* what I feel," I told them, stopping again. "That's the whole problem. In his own way, Ben has expressed that he... wants us to be involved. *Seriously* involved. And I just... in the back of my mind, it's like I'm cheating on Jay."

My mother shook her head. "It has been *two years*, sweetheart. Of course I'm not saying you should be 'over it', or that you should do something you aren't ready to do. But this guilt, this... sense of lingering duty... you have to let that go. Let it all go. Live a life you haven't lived before. Isn't that something like what your little smart-mouthed ass said to me on the phone the other day?"

"Maybe, but *wow*," I said, eyes wide. "Aggressive much?"

"I'm saying, *geez*, mama," Jude added, laughing.

"I have to make sure you know I noticed," Mama said, with a wink. "But back to my point – there's nothing wrong with wanting companionship again. No one expects you to be some lonesome widow for the rest of your life. Jay would want you to be happy – and so would Nova. You gave them *so much*. When they were gone, you gave that hospital *so much*. Now, it's time to pour all that back into *yourself*."

By the time she finished, I had tears in my eyes. They must've known I needed it, because before I could ask, my mom and sister had crowded me into a hug.

"Now," my mother said, once we'd pulled back. "Tell me about this *Ben*. I want to know everything there is to know. How did you meet him?"

I exchanged a look with Jude, who smirked.

"Well... that's a bit of an interesting story..."

While I told it, we kept walking, detouring at the battered, faded *Honey Branch Winery and Vineyard* sign I'd passed many times, but never explored. It was a big, sprawling property, with what seemed like miles of overgrown vineyard space, anchored by two main buildings and then a charming little house up on another hill. More of the mountain range extended into the area behind the property, creating a gorgeous view.

"Well this is pretty, isn't it?" my mother asked, as we stopped on a hill to look around. None of us were sure this was public property, so we weren't venturing further.

"I think the family who owns it is still around here somewhere. I hate that this has all gone into disrepair though. Maple carries their wine, and it's honestly amazing stuff."

"Isn't there a thing about the higher altitude making better grapes, which makes better wine?" Jude asked, and I nodded.

"I feel like I've heard that before too. But I don't know anything about wine other than that it tastes good."

"And will have you ready to climb the man that served it to you," my mother added, sending us all into a fit of laughter.

We were still laughing when we realized we weren't the only ones with the idea of visiting the property – there were two people headed towards us, and I quickly realized one was Justine, from the doctor's office.

"Hey, Kyle," she greeted with a hug, once they'd made it to where we were. "This is my friend, Eva. Eva is a complete lush, and about to buy this property," she added, gesturing toward the beautiful mahogany-skinned woman standing beside her, who rolled her eyes.

"You make me sick," she told Justine, then turned to me. "It's lovely to meet you Kyle. Ignore my friend. Her mother dropped her as a baby."

"Doris will fight you," Justine countered, which made my eyes go wide.

"Wait, Doris Jones, who runs the diner is your mother?" I asked. "How did I not know that?"

"Not asking the right questions I guess," Justine laughed. "Chief Chisolm is my father – well, the only one I've ever known. I have my birth father's last name, since I can already see the question spinning in your head."

"Thank you, because I was certainly about to ask how you ended up an Ellis," I teased. "Eva, Justine, this is *my* mother, Cookie, and my sister, Jude."

"You're thinking about buying this place, is that what I heard?" my mother asked, once the usual greetings had been exchanged. "See, this young woman is doing real things with her money," she added, looking pointedly at Jude and me. "What do you do for a living?"

Eva laughed. "Collect alimony checks and troll my ex-husband on social media."

My mother's mouth dropped, and Jude burst into giggles. "Now see?" she chided my mother. "That's what happens when you don't mind your business. Good for you though girl, that honestly sounds amazing," she told Eva, who nodded.

"It is. It really, *really* is."

Of course after that, my mother was ready to go before Jude got any ideas – not that she was leaving Davis for anything – but Jude and I took our time with the goodbyes, before we headed on into town.

Along the way, we kept running into people I'd become acquainted with in my time in Sugar Valley, which... was damn near everybody.

"You've settled in here, haven't you?" my mother asked in awe after a firetruck driven by Todd – Ben's cousin – had stopped in the middle of the road so he and Marc could flirt with us.

I tipped my head to the side, thinking about it. "Yeah... I guess I kinda have."

"To be expected. You've been here what, almost three months?" Jude said. "You thinking about letting Blackwood go?"

"She most certainly is *not*," my mother gasped, staring at Jude like she'd sprouted a second head. "Are you?"

Averting my gaze, I focused intently on a half-faded chalk drawing some child had left behind. It was a good one – a purple sun setting over a green mountain, with a bright white sky. I had a box full of Nova's old drawings that looked like this, somewhere.

"I don't know. Maybe. Probably." I finally turned back to my mother, who looked dazed, but all I could do was shrug. "I have Nova and Jay with me every day now, in my heart. At some point, every single day, I look at their faces. They're recommitted to my memories now, and I can still breathe. *Here*. I don't know if I can breathe in that house – in *our* house – anymore."

"So buy a new house," Mama chimed, as if it were such a simple solution. "We'll pack it up for you. You can put their things in storage, keep them as long as you need to. But you *belong* at home."

I groaned. "Are we starting this again?"

"If you're talking about moving here permanently, you're damn right we are!"

"Didn't we talk about this already Mama?" Jude slipped in. "I thought I prepared you for this?"

"I'm not prepared to do anything but take my ass back to civilization – bringing *both* my children with me!" my mother snapped, then turned to walk off alone. Jude and I both knew better than to fight it too hard when she got into one of her moods, and if we didn't, *I* wasn't in the mood for the shenanigans. I hadn't even given it enough thought to make a final decision anyway.

Arguing about it was pointless.

We caught up to her outside the clinic where she'd apparently stopped Lilah to ask about her shoes. If nothing else, that was a definite perk of not working emergency services – if you wanted, you could wear cute clothes, even heels.

From what I could tell, Lilah had a collection to envy.

"Hey Kyle," Lilah greeted as she straightened from pointing out something about the straps on her heel to my mother. "Please wish me luck, I'm heading out to an interview."

My eyes widened. "Interview? So you found someone to take over?"

"A few strong candidates, but…" her nose wrinkled. "None I'm in love with. But, I figure I shouldn't let that stop me from keeping the ball rolling. There's an opening at Blackwood General."

"Not my daughter's, I hope?!" Mama chimed in, loud and wrong.

"Lilah isn't a surgeon, Mama. She practices family medicine."

"Right," Lilah added. "I'm trying to get to Blackwood to learn what Kyle already knows… *Mama?*"

I chuckled. "Yes. This is my mother, and my sister. They… popped up for a visit today."

"Oh how *nice*," Lilah gushed. "It's lovely to meet both of you! You must be so proud of Kyle."

"*Hmph.* Maybe when she's not trying to break my heart by staying in this little Hallmark town instead of bringing her ass home."

"*Can you relax?*" Jude and I hissed, at the same time, but Lilah only seemed interested in a specific part of my mother's grousing.

"Staying in town? *Really?!*" she squeaked as my mother sulked off. "Does that mean you'll be putting your name in the ring to take over the clinic?!"

"It doesn't, I'm sorry," I told her, feeling bad when her excitement deflated. "I truly don't know how much longer I'll be here, so I wouldn't want to make a commitment like that."

Lilah sighed. "I understand. Well... it'll be a few weeks before I have to make a final decision, so if something changes between now and then..."

"I will absolutely let you know. Thank you, so much. And good luck with your interview, okay? If you need a reference, I'll gladly give you one."

Her eyes lit up again. "Really?"

"Of course, Lilah. You're a great doctor."

Wearing a broad smile, she nodded. "Thank you. I'll let you know how it goes."

Once she was gone, Jude spoke up.

"She seemed sweet. Bubbly."

I sighed. "Yeah, and she's probably going to *lose* some of that bubble when she finds out about Ben and me."

"They used to date?"

"She asked him out. He laughed, because she's entirely too nice for him."

"He's an asshole."

"Yep. Makes me pretty mad."

Jude grinned. "I think it's a good vibe for you. Maybe not before, but definitely now. You look... happy. The mountains have been good to you, big sis."

I returned her smile. "Yeah. They have."

"Wʜᴀᴛ'ᴅ you do to my wife?" my father asked, taking a seat beside me outside the family lodge they'd booked for the night. Jude had wanted to see the fire pit, so of course Davis had made it happen for her, and now they were cuddled up together, whispering and kissing. My nephew, DJ, had fallen asleep across my lap.

I accepted the beer he handed me and sighed, shaking my head. Mama was inside somewhere, still sulking about earlier.

"Asserted myself as an adult," I answered my father's question. "You know she hates that."

He chuckled and took a swig. "Ah, yeah. She stopped short of claiming you and Chip jumped on her when she was explaining it all."

"Sounds about right."

For a few moments, neither of us said anything, and then, "You alright up here Doodle?"

I tried my level best not to smile at the nickname I'd been given – "Snicker doodle", because of my cinnamon-toned skin. Jude was "Chip" – but I couldn't help myself. "Yeah, Daddy. I'm fine. Why?"

He motioned at DJ in my lap, then across to where Jude and Davis were looking... something way more profound than in love with each other. I realized what he was asking – if being surrounded by what I'd lost was triggering. His concern was warming.

"I'm good," I assured him, running a hand over DJ's soft waves. I'd never, *ever* begrudged the fullness of Jude's life. DJ and Nova had loved each other dearly, even with their age difference. He was another place for her memory to live on – one of so many things I treasured about him.

There was lots of violence available for consumption, in movies, books, and on TV. One particularly frustrating thing was the trivialization of a gunshot wound – the immense destruction it wreaked on an adult body.

In a child?

That was a very, *very* particular type of hell to attempt to mitigate.

I couldn't come away from an experience like that not appreciating the inherent light and innocence of children.

Especially my DJ.

Nobody, not even Jude, knew this, but he was the reason I'd left Blackwood. Davis was out of town, Jude had an early emergency appointment, and they needed someone to take DJ to school.

Of course Auntie Kyle could do it.

I didn't have to be at the hospital until later that day, so we sang our ABCs, and talked about the latest cartoons, and what he wanted his mommy to make for dinner that day. It was sweet, like moments with him always were. If anybody could get energy from me, it was my DJ.

But then, as I waited in line to drop him off, he asked the most straightforward, most innocent question, that... absolutely shattered me.

"Auntie Kyle?"

I met his eyes in the rearview mirror and smiled. "Yes, baby?"

"I miss SuperNova and Uncle Jay. Are they coming back from Heaven soon?"

I shifted the car into park, and he reflexively unstrapped from his booster seat as one of the drop-off attendants came to open the door. But he didn't move to leave the car. Wasn't moving until I answered.

I shook my head. "No, baby. They aren't."

"Oh..." he pouted. "Okay."

And then he was off.

Running to meet up with his friends who'd just climbed out of cars too. The principal was outside today – the same principal Nova had when she was at this school for elementary – and she waved to me, recognition bringing a mournful smile to her lips as I drove away.

I considered driving off a bridge.

No one knew that part, either.

Instead, I drove home and turned off my phone, turned off all the lights, and climbed into my bed.

I stayed there until the next day, when I booked my trip to Sugar Valley.

"This seems like a nice place to make a living," my father said, pulling me from my thoughts.

I shook my head. "Why is everybody assuming I plan to stay?"

"Well, I can't speak for everybody, but I don't see why you *wouldn't*. Nice fresh air, it's safe, you've got everything you need right there in town. And... your *friend* is here."

I frowned. "My friend... *Ben?*"

He nodded.

"Oh. That's... an interesting thing to call him."

"Is he not?" my father pressed. "You two sure seemed pretty *friendly* to me."

"Oh *geeeeeez* Daddy," I groaned, making him laugh.

"You're a grown woman now, Doodle. Coming up on forty before you know it. Not shit to be embarrassed about – and he seems like a decent guy."

My eyebrows shot up. "What gave you that impression? Answering the door in his boxers, or smacking me on the ass?"

He laughed. "That was the type of thing I would've done to your Mama. Unnecessary flexing to make sure your granddaddy knew I wasn't scared of his ass."

"Oh is *that* what that was?"

"Game recognize game, baby girl."

"Wow," I chuckled. "I can't with you right now. Arrogance is your bonding point with him?"

He shook his head. "Nah. A perfectly cooked steak is."

"Excuse me?"

"We ran into him up on the mountain. Me and Davis and DJ. He showed us out to his house, put some steaks on the grill. A *charcoal* grill, like a real man."

"Oh *God*," I groaned, rolling my eyes. "You're serious?"

"Dead serious."

"*Wow*. Wow. What on earth did you talk about?"

He smiled. "You."

"*Me?!*"

"Why do you sound so surprised?"

I blinked. "I... if you understood the... *journey* that it took for he and I to even be cordial, you'd understand why him cooking a steak for my father and wanting to talk about me is like... twilight zone material."

"Well, he mentioned that there was a rocky start, but Doodle... that's just the start. It's not abnormal for the man to want to know about you from the people who love you. And don't worry – we didn't tell him anything too bad. Your nephew *did* spill the beans about that time Jay made you laugh so hard you threw up though."

I narrowed my eyes at his talkative little ass, snoring against my legs. "Mmmhmm, he gets *that* from his mama."

Daddy laughed. "Don't stress it, okay? It probably sounds more serious to you than it was for any of us."

"Of course it does. None of you have to take it as seriously as I do."

"The hell we don't," he argued. "You're *my* child, and grown or not, I expect a certain standard. Even with that little show he put on when we arrived, he fessed up to saying something out of line to you. He didn't tell me the specifics, and I don't want to know – but he said something that earned my respect. Something I plan to hold him to."

My lips parted. "Okay... what exactly was it?"

"That he'd hurt you. That he was sorry for it. And that it

would never happen again," my father concluded, sitting back. "Long as he stays with that, the man is alright with me."

"Really... he said that?"

Daddy nodded. "He said that."

"Wow. I... don't even know what to say." I stared into the fire, trying to process. "Maybe two weeks ago, his mother told me about how... after he lost his father, Ben kinda... clammed up. He froze. Which I can deeply relate to. He managed to come out of that, but then he lost someone else, and it happened again. He froze. And so... I guess I don't understand how he can be so open and welcoming with you."

My father pushed out a sigh. "It's... human nature. We're all hard wired to want what we don't have. I didn't need you to tell me that boy had lost his father. I felt it. He realized I liked outdoors, and we could talk fishing and have a beer and eat a steak... I bet he had the same things in common with his own father."

"But—"

"Let me finish my point now," he said, waving me off. "Well, this is actually a different one, but... look at you up here. Your mother told me everybody in this little town knows you. *Loves* you. That true?"

I shrugged. "I don't know about the *love* part, but yeah. The people here are great from what I can tell."

"Because you've talked to them. Got to know them. Shared meals with them?"

"Sure," I nodded. "But...?"

"You don't see where I'm taking this?" he chuckled. "You said yourself, you related to being numb, and frozen after a loss. You were in that state a *long* time. But now look where you are – happy. *Connected.* Seems like being here unlocked something for you. And maybe your being here... unlocked something for him too."

After that, we were interrupted by Davis and Jude coming to collect DJ to take him to bed. I exchanged good nights with them, then went inside to kiss my mother, who was still on her silent treatment nonsense, but would be fine tomorrow.

She told me so.

I insisted on going back to my own cabin for the night, so my father walked out to the porch with me, where he could see me the entire way.

"Just think about what I said, okay?" he insisted, and I agreed before bidding him goodnight, and starting the short walk... "home".

Ben was on my doorstep, waiting.

"You know you're freaking me out, right?" I asked, as soon as I was close enough for him to hear me.

He grinned.

Damn he's fine.

"My bad. I'm not familiar with the proper protocols and all that, so... you'll have to excuse me."

I stopped in front of him. "And if I don't?"

"I said you *have* to though. So you *have* to."

I laughed. "Whatever. It's cold. You coming inside or not?" I asked, stepping past him to get to the door.

"Hell yeah I'm coming inside. And then I'm *coming* inside too."

CHAPTER THIRTEEN

"Wow. So I finally get a plate saved now?"

Mama laughed at me as she took a seat across from me at the table – no plate, just tea for her. "I wish you'd quit acting like I threw you away or something."

"That makes two of us," I countered, tucking into the plate of baked chicken, greens, yams, and macaroni. I couldn't tell if it had just been a while, or if she'd *really* put her foot in the meal this time.

Either way, it was *fire*.

"I have something to talk to you about."

Mouth full of food, I stopped chewing, looking up from my plate to meet my mother's gaze. "I should've known this was too good to be true." I swallowed. "What's up? What's wrong?"

"Nothing's wrong. Nothing at all." She had this weird smile on her face that kept me from filling my fork again.

"Okay, well... then what is this about?"

My mother took a deep breath, then tucked her hands into her lap as her smile changed. "I heard you made a good impression with Kyle's family."

"Don't change the subject," I told her, shaking my head. "You didn't serve me *this* to talk about Kyle. And I already spotted that caramel cake on the counter, so... it must be big. It must be fuc—messed up. *Really* messed up. So go ahead and tell me."

She pushed out a sigh, then shifted her hands again, laying them flat on the table. When she didn't say anything, I frowned, ready to threaten leaving. But then, she moved her fingers and something caught my eye.

Something sparkling.

Lustrous, and big, reflecting off the overhead light.

"Wow. *Wow*," I said, pushing back from the table. "*Wow*."

"Benny, don't—"

"You're *marrying* that mother—"

"*Benny*. I will *not* tolerate you disrespecting him right in front of me. It's been long enough that—"

"It *hasn't* been long enough," I interjected, standing up. "It will *never* be long enough for me to be cool with you and... *him*. He was my father's *best friend*. I won't accept him. I'll never accept him."

"So you get to move on?" she asked, coming to her feet as well. "Just you? We lost Ben almost *twenty* years ago. I don't get to find new love?"

I shook my head. "It's not about that, Mama! Of course I don't want you to be alone, I want you be happy."

"I *am* happy."

"*Why him?*" I backed away from the table, glancing at my forgotten plate. My appetite was *gone* now, courtesy of the rock – the *engagement ring* – on my mother's finger. "I never... I've never questioned you, about that. You're my mother, you're grown. It's not my place to question, but... him?!"

"We were *all* friends, Benny! I've known Henry forever.

Loved him forever, even when it wasn't romantic. After your father died—"

"He was *married*. To your friend!"

She shook her head. "I mean *way* after. After he and Doris divorced. We talked. We got close again. And now... yes, *him*. He asked, and I said yes, and I'd like you to be there. Just a small thing."

"That's never happening." I shrugged, looking away so I wouldn't have to see the hurt in her eyes. "I won't support that. I *can't* support that."

Mama threw her hands up. "Why? Why can't you?"

"Because, do you *not* see how messed up this is? Two men go into a fire, only one comes back. That one gets to marry the other one's wife. That sounds right to you? Was he plotting that shit from the beginning?"

"Benny, that is ridiculous."

"Is it?!" I asked, frowning. "Does Doris know about this? The relationship hasn't been secret, but this... engagement mess?"

One arched eyebrow lifted. "You will kindly *not* refer to my engagement as 'mess'. And... no. Doris removed herself from the *Regina's Business* newsletter."

"Can you blame her for being mad that her best friend started seeing her ex-husband!?"

"*Yes*," Mama hissed, stepping toward me with her finger pointed. "I knew him first!"

"That's your defense? Really?"

She nodded, nostrils flared. "It sure as hell is, son, and let me tell you something – you may want to make sure you know the whole story before you go worrying too much about Doris' feelings – or your late father's, for that matter."

"Whole story?"

"Oh yes. You see, when I say I knew Henry first, I mean I *knew* Henry first. I dropped him way back then, for your father. And I *never* begrudged Doris for dating him after me – he was a good man then, and he still is now."

I sucked my teeth. "So the rumors about Doris and Henry breaking up because of infidelity, that's all just pulled from the sky?"

"More like pulled out of her ass," Mama countered. "Like I said, you're so worried about Doris and your father, maybe I should've been worried too."

My head snapped back. "*What?*"

"Oh you heard me right. See, you remember about six or seven years back, Doris had breast cancer?"

"Yeah, of course. The whole town did a fundraiser for her treatments and all that."

"Mmmmhmmm." My mother rolled her eyes. "That trollop thought she was done with her time in the land of the living, so she decided she was going to make her amends. She wanted to *confess.*"

"Are you saying...."

"*Mmmhmm.*"

I put my weight against the counter for support, shaking my head. "I... you never said anything about it..."

"Why would I?" she asked. "I don't now, and never have had any interest in ruining your view of your father. And I don't harbor any ill feelings toward him for a thirty-some-odd-year old infidelity. Against Doris either for that matter."

"You just called her a... *trollop*... though."

"And I'll call her one to her face too, any damn time I please. That doesn't mean I haven't forgiven her – hell, we repaired our friendship again *after* she told me that! And now, she has the nerve to be upset that I returned to what was mine in the first damn place. But *anyhow*, my point is that... I'm not concerned with Doris' feelings. And you can stop acting like a petulant child toward Henry cause you think you're defending your father's memory."

Once again, I shook my head. It felt like the only thing to do with this flood of new information coming to me.

My *father*?

A *cheater*?

There was no possible way, not the way I'd seen him look at my mother, not the way he loved her, loved his family. I wasn't so naïve to think that nobody did it – I'd seen plenty of guys risk relationships they claimed to cherish for pussy – but I never understood it. It wasn't even that I had some deep moral opposition, I just thought the shit was stupid.

I thought my father thought it was stupid.

I thought we were just wired differently.

But apparently not.

"I'm sorry, if I've shattered your perfect illusion of your father, Benny. But understand that, even with what I just told you, I loved your father, *dearly*. And I still treasure his memory. The timing that the... indiscretion occurred... it was a rough time for us. We both made mistakes. That's all I'll say to that, and more than you need to know, I just... I needed you to understand *why* I am where I am with this. I feel completely free wearing Henry's ring, and I am... *so* happy. I hope you can find it in yourself to be happy for me."

I pushed out a sigh, dropping my gaze again. While I understood where *she* was coming from, and wasn't even trying to hold the shit against her... I wasn't yet at a place where Chief Chisolm was even remotely square by me, not when it came to this.

"I'm gonna go, aiight?"

She let out a deep breath. "Okay son. Leave me my grandbaby," she said, glancing at Domino, who'd already curled up by the fireplace and gone to sleep.

"Yes ma'am," I told her, hobbling over to where she stood to give her a hug. I was trying now to only use my crutches outdoors, so my path was awkward, but she welcomed me, as always, with open arms. "I love you," I told her as she squeezed me tight, and I returned the embrace.

"I love you too Benny."

Ten minutes later I was still pissed, sitting in the parking lot behind the lodges. After a few seconds of debate, I turned the truck off, then made my way to Kyle's door.

It didn't take her long to answer, and she did so in nothing but an oversized sweater – the same sweater she'd worn to bring me dinner that day, weeks ago. A sweater I'd seen a lot since then.

Her favorite.

"Hi," she said, her pretty lips turned up into a smile. "Sorry to disappoint, but I didn't fix a meal today. I had dinner at Maple."

I shrugged. "I didn't come for that anyway."

"I'm not in a sexy mood."

"What?" I frowned. "I thought we established that we were off that. Or... *on* more than that... or something. Whatever. You know what I'm saying."

She laughed. "Yeah, I guess. But I also haven't seen you since then, and it's been like three days."

"Really?" I asked, like I didn't already know exactly how long it had been, down to the hour. My comfort level with her family had messed with my head a little, honestly, and I'd wondered if distance would help.

It hadn't.

It made me antsy.

"Come in," she said, stepping back. "It's cold out."

I did, closing the door behind me. I'd barely turned the lock when I realized something about the space was... off.

It was too clean.

Not that it was usually messy, but there were none of the signs I'd grown used to that Kyle lived there. No boots or jackets by the door, no blanket draped over the couch.

"What's going on," I asked, stopping her path to her bedroom. "Where's all your stuff?"

Her eyes widened. "Oh, um... I'm packing. To leave. I'm leaving tomorrow."

"You... *what?*"

She crossed her arms as she leaned against the wall. "I need to go back to Blackwood. Check in on my house, and talk to my boss... decide what I'm going to do."

"And you just... you were gonna leave without saying anything?"

Kyle frowned. "What? *No.*"

"That's exactly what it looks like."

"That doesn't make it reality." She pointed to the counter, where I noticed a covered glass baking dish. "That is a peach cobbler that I planned to drop by your house with tonight."

I chuckled. "A peach cobbler was going to make it okay that you were leaving without any notice?"

"No, a peach cobbler was supposed to convince you to come with me. If you could get away, for a day or two. Maybe? I don't want to go alone."

"Isn't your family in Blackwood?"

"I don't want to go alone," she repeated, not breaking our gaze. "If you can't, it's—"

"I'll go with you." I nodded. "It's not a problem. I could probably use a little break from Sugar Valley anyway."

Her head shifted to the side. "Really? Why? Did something happen?"

I sighed. Usually, this would be the place where I brushed whoever I was talking to off, swallowing whatever it was until it went away. But Kyle's attentive, big brown eyes made it hard to tap into that default reaction. When I didn't say anything, she stepped forward, concerned, looking me right in the face, waiting.

So...

Fuck it.

I told her.

We sat there on the couch, and I told her everything, shit I'd never expressed out loud about how much Chief Chisolm's whole existence agitated me. We'd been fine until the fire that took Devin. After that, I had to keep my distance. When he started up with my mother last year – something I immediately knew about, even though they tried to hide it – I hadn't been happy.

At all.

But he was a good fire chief.

He'd been my father's good friend.

As far as I knew, he was a good person.

I tried, my very best, to let my professional respect for him overrule my personal feelings, and thus far... I'd been cool.

But *marrying my mother?*

This shit wasn't cool.

"I guess I don't understand the big deal?" Kyle said, once I'd finished. "Well, wait, because that sounds dismissive, and that's not what I mean. What I'm saying is... I understand everything you're saying. Understand your frustrations. What I *don't* understand is why your mother's happiness doesn't overrule that. Regina is what, in her sixties? She's lived enough life to be able to do whatever the hell she wants, and as long as she's not harming herself or anybody else... this isn't what you want to hear, but you have to swallow it. She's not asking you to call this man Daddy – she's asking for an hour of your time, as the most important person in her life, to stand by her side as she commits to the man she loves."

I scoffed. "So if it were you, you'd go? You'd support this? You'd be cool with it?"

"Ben... my mother has 'fresh from the oven' tattooed, in kanji, on her inner thigh. I sat in the tattoo shop with her while she got it. I held her hand. Because she asked me to, and she's my mother, and she's not hurting anybody, and it made her *happy*. If I can do that, which is arguably worse... you can trust your mother with the man your father called his best friend. You can be pissed about it, in your head. But you can damn sure do it."

I pushed out a deep sigh, leaning back against the couch to look at the ceiling. She was right, but still... I didn't like this shit.

I didn't like it at all.

"Call her," Kyle said, standing up. "I need to finish packing."

I frowned. "What, right now?"

"Yeah, right now," she agreed. "Barring some type of abuse, a man that isn't right with his mama will *never* be right with me, so... get it done. Tell her you'll be there."

I groaned. "Can I taste the peach cobbler first?"

"You're not tasting *anything* around here until you handle your business."

With that, she left me on the couch, disappearing around the corner to her room.

And I... pulled my phone from my pocket.

"Better had," Kyle said, and I looked up to see her peeking around the corner as I put the phone to my ear.

I didn't get a chance to counter that, because my mother answered, with enough emotion in her voice that I knew I'd made the right call. The peach cobbler smelled good, sure, but... I would've called anyway.

"Everything okay son?" she asked, and I took a deep breath.

"Yeah, but... we need to talk."

I WAS JUST COMING to look, I swear.

It was coming up on four months since I left Blackwood, and no one except the cleaning service had been inside since then – it *needed* to be checked on.

Or maybe that was my excuse.

Maybe I was here to see if I could handle it – see if I could be in this space, still so ripe with memories of Nova and Jay.

I... couldn't.

That was how I ended up on the phone with a packing service, hiring whoever could send someone immediately. Their instructions were to take everything – *everything*. Donate all the clothes and shoes to local shelters, anything in the pantries to the food bank. The furniture and appliances could stay – the realtor I called, she liked the idea. Wanted to come see the place.

Fine.

I was letting it all go.

All except this one box.

I'd snagged an empty one from the packers, using it to collect the private things. Nova's journals, and her laptop, the awards from her room, and her favorite stuffed animal that she'd had since she was a baby. I did the same for Jay, except instead of journals, his father's shaving kit that he never used, passed down from generation to generation. I'd send it to his brother. He didn't have children yet, but he might.

Eventually, I would wipe their laptops clean of their personal information. Or I never would – I was certainly never opening Nova's journals. To the box, I added my own things that I might want to look at again someday, but had no use for now. If I hadn't needed it in four months, it was probably safe to call it disposable. Only the things in this specific box were not.

I filled it, and then I taped it closed.

And *then*, I let myself cry the tears I'd been holding back all day.

Ben probably thought I was crazy, and... maybe he was right. He hadn't said much, but he'd been hanging close, making sure I had what I needed. And when it was all done, he let me use his shoulder.

"I'm glad you came with me," I told him, once everyone had left. We'd ordered hibachi takeout, and were sitting out on the floor in the living room, eating everything straight from the styrofoam containers. If I didn't think about it too hard, it almost felt like I was back in Sugar Valley. "We should probably head to the hotel and get some sleep. Get ready for tomorrow."

He swallowed the mouthful he was chewing, and then asked, "What's happening tomorrow?"

"My *mother* is happening tomorrow," I answered, then chuckled. "You only saw her in passing when they came up. So like I said, get ready. I'm going to introduce you to a *real* stunt queen."

It wasn't as if my decision to sell the house would come as a surprise. A permanent move to Sugar Valley was already a foregone conclusion to pretty much everyone except me. My mother was the only one who seemed to think it was a bad idea, but she felt that about anything that supposedly drove me further away from her.

"You saying my mother is lightweight compared to her?"

I laughed. "Oh, absolutely. *Absolutely.*"

"Keep that energy when she's micromanaging what you wear to this goddamn wedding."

"Wedding?!" my eyes bucked. "I thought they were doing the courthouse thing, she wants a full-blown *wedding* now?"

He nodded. "Yep. Your fault. Now that *I'm* on board... she wants the whole shebang."

I laughed, shaking my head. "Good for her. With everything that's happened, it would be easy for her to give up on this whole love thing. But she didn't. It's inspirational."

Ben groaned. "Inspirational? Ah, damn, don't tell me you're going to be wanting a wedding next."

"A wedding to get married to *who*?!" I asked, almost choking on a mouthful of broccoli.

"I'm not a catch now? Is that what you're trying to imply?"

"I'm not *implying* anything, I'm stating right now, for the record, that it'll be a long time before – if *ever* – I'm ready to consider marriage. And while we're here... I want to remind you... I can't give you babies. So if either of those are deal breakers..."

"Legal marriage contracts and children are two of the things that make it hardest to get rid of somebody when you're tired of their ass, and you think that might be a deal breaker. *For me?* Damn, you don't know me, do you?"

I threw a piece of zucchini, popping him right in the eyebrow. "I'm trying to be serious."

"So am *I*," he countered, getting me back with a chunk of fried egg from his rice. "I'm out here trying to be reassuring, and you think I'm playing."

"Sorry if your talk of keeping it easy to get rid of me doesn't exactly inspire confidence."

He blew out a sigh, then set his takeout container to the side and put his fork down. "Come here."

My eyebrow raised for a moment, and then I turned my attention back to my own rice, picking through it to find another shrimp. "What?"

"I said *come here*," he repeated, motioning for me to put my food down. I grew even *more* confused when he patted his lap.

"For what?"

"Woman, if you don't bring your ass…"

"*Ugh.* Fine," I muttered, putting my food down to crawl over to him. We had already been close, legs stretched for comfort, but as soon as I got near, he pulled me between his legs, wrapping his arms around me from behind, holding me close.

He'd never held me like this before.

We'd come about in such an unconventional way that we'd sexed each other about twenty different ways, but had never experienced the basic intimacy of cuddling. I couldn't help feeling that we'd been missing out, because it felt… amazing, honestly. His arms around me, the heat of his body against my back, his lips on my neck. I closed my eyes, relishing something I hadn't had in a long, *long* time.

Not since—

"Do you feel better now?" he asked, curving himself around me to speak into my ear.

I took a second to consider it, then nodded as a contended

sigh pressed from my lips. "Yes, actually. But I also don't even remember what we were talking about, so... yeah. There's that."

The warm rumble of Ben's laugh vibrated through me. "I think you were using your perceived flaws to try to scare me off or something. Didn't work though."

"Shit," I replied. "Okay, tell me yours, so maybe you'll scare *me* off."

"Uh... I'm a well-established and documented asshole, but you already knew that. And... I'm relentless, which can be a pretty major flaw. Once I decide I'm doing something, or want something, even if I know it's a bad idea... I can't stop myself. I'm doing it. I'm getting it. I'm going into the burning building. I'm getting the clumsy ass girl who fell off the mountain."

I twisted in his arms, to see his face. "That's what you think? That you've *got me*?"

"Don't I?" he asked, leaning in to press his lips to mine.

"I still haven't *officially* moved to Sugar Valley yet. I don't even have my own place."

He bit his lip. "You better get on that, because you can't stay with me."

"I wasn't trying to shack up with you *anyway*, ew!" I laughed. "It was a commentary on me having a lot to do when I get back. Ask Lilah about the job, look for a place..."

"Yeah, sure. Good save."

"It's not a *save*."

"If you say so."

I closed my eyes again as he buried his face in my neck, breathing me in. It was probably strange, but something about that subtle act put me even more at ease than I already was.

More at ease than I'd been in what felt like forever.

Real peace.

The very thing I'd set out to find in the first place.

"TWO ROADS DIVERGED IN A... GREEN WOOD," I muttered to myself, stopping at a break in the heavily wooded path. It was summer now, so the foliage was still vivid green, and thick enough to provide cover from the beaming sun. There weren't *roads,* not exactly. There was one densely grown trail on the left, and another on the right, both calling to me with a chorus of birds and bugs, both illuminated by bright yellow sunlight peeking through the canopy.

A decision to make.

Which was fine.

I knew *exactly* where I was going.

"Bring that ass, Desmond," Ben called, smacking me on the ass he'd requested I bring as he passed me, taking the path that would lead us further up the mountain. Domino followed shortly behind, taking the time to run a few circles around me before she caught up to Ben.

I took a long swig from my water, and then kept moving.

It wasn't hard to keep up with Ben, with his healing injury still slowing him down. Even with that, we were making good time, passing the place I'd stopped to take that ill-fated selfie, then the spot where I'd run into him on my birthday hike, and then finally... the peak.

I hadn't done this when I came by myself, for fear I wouldn't be able to get back out, but with Ben and Domino, I climbed over the ragged edge of the crater, reaching the actual lake. There was a wide, sturdy rock shelf there, where a few people were resting, dipping toes into the water, taking pictures.

I wanted to do all that too.

Under threat of physical harm, I got Ben into a picture with Domino and me. It took a threat of withholding pussy to get a supposed smile, that looked more like a grimace when I reviewed the image, but it was fine.

It was enough.

I just wanted something to ground the memory.

Such a *good* memory.

We'd brought food, so we stayed there at the crater lake, to eat, and talk, and play with Domino. We laughed, and went back and forth, and he said something that hit the boundary of "too far", so I did too, and then we both apologized and decided we'd been out long enough.

The sun was starting to go down.

It was time to get back to his place, and have makeup sex, even though we'd already made up.

"Just one more picture first," I insisted, once we'd climbed out of the crater.

"You mean a hundred, until you get the perfect one," Ben complained, frowning. "Don't you start at the clinic in the morning. I'm ready to put you to bed, so you can get some rest."

"You'll get your pussy, relax," I told him, waving him off as I moved around, looking at my cell phone screen to determine the best angle. "It'll only take a second."

"Cool, I'll meet you back at my place."

"If you leave without me, I'm going to *my* house, not yours," I called to his retreating back. He stopped, groaning.

"Take the damn picture, woman."

"Shut up, I'm trying!"

I grinned at myself in my camera, satisfied with what I saw. My eyes no longer carried the loneliness and desolation I'd seen in the selfie I'd taken down at the waterfall the day I arrived. I was a becoming a different woman, not for the first time in my life.

This one was happy.

I snapped the picture, then slipped the phone into my pocket.

"There," I said, smirking at Ben. "Just *one*, and it's perfect, how about tha—*Ahhh!*"

My hands clutched at empty air as my boots slid from under me and I fell backward, into the crater we'd just climbed out of.

"*Goddamnit, Kyle!*" I heard Ben grumble.

Luckily for me, it was a pretty short fall, that my backpack took the brunt of.

It still hurt like a bitch though.

I peeled the backpack off, laying out on my back in time to see Ben and Domino peeking over the crater.

"Are you okay?" he asked, his voice full of concern.

I nodded. "Yeah. Just knocked the wind out of me. I'm good."

By the time he climbed down, I'd made my way back to my feet, and was reaching to return my backpack to my shoulders.

"You sure you're okay?" he questioned, looking me over.

"*Yes*," I insisted. "I'm fine."

"Good," he replied, sounding relieved. "That means it's okay for me to do this."

I frowned, confused, but just for a second. Immediately after that, I was rolling my eyes as he let out a deep, eye-watering roar of laughter that soon had him doubled over, clutching his stomach.

And then... because I couldn't help it, I was laughing too.

This was it.

This moment right here, was everything the last several months had been leading up to.

Hurting, but still able to laugh through it.

Exhausted, but ready to see what was next.

Grieving... but finally able to see the possibility of something else on the horizon.

I grinned as Ben wrapped his arms around me for a hug, pulling me in tight.

"I'm glad you're okay," he muttered into my ear. "Clumsy ass."

He pulled away, motioning for me to follow him so we could climb out of the crater again. This time, there was no fear – my steps were sure, and I was confident in my destination.

Missteps aside, I'd gotten damned good at climbing mountains.

ACKNOWLEDGMENTS

Thank you, God, for the gift of storytelling and a colorful imagination. Both have gotten me through a lot.

To my family – husband, kids, friends – thank you for understanding, patience, and a bottomless well of support.

To those who have provided feedback through this project, thank you for your strong opinions and kind words along the way.

To my readers, I can't say thank you enough for affirming that Black love has always been, is, and will always be, in style. Not a trend, or a fad. Here to stay.

Thank you.

~

ABOUT THE AUTHOR

christina c jones

love, in warm hues

Christina C. Jones is a modern romance novelist who has penned many love stories. She has earned a reputation as a storyteller who seamlessly weaves the complexities of modern life into captivating tales of black romance.

ALSO BY CHRISTINA C JONES

Love and Other Things

Haunted (paranormal)

Mine Tonight (erotica)

Equilibrium

Love Notes

Five Start Enterprises

Anonymous Acts

More Than a Hashtag

Relationship Goals

High Stakes

Ante Up

King of Hearts

Deuces Wild

Sweet Heat

Hints of Spice (Highlight Reel spinoff)

A Dash of Heat

A Touch of Sugar

Truth, Lies, and Consequences

The Truth – His Side, Her Side, And the Truth About Falling In Love

The Lies – The Lies We Tell About Life, Love, and Everything in Between

Friends & Lovers:

Made in the USA
Columbia, SC
27 May 2021